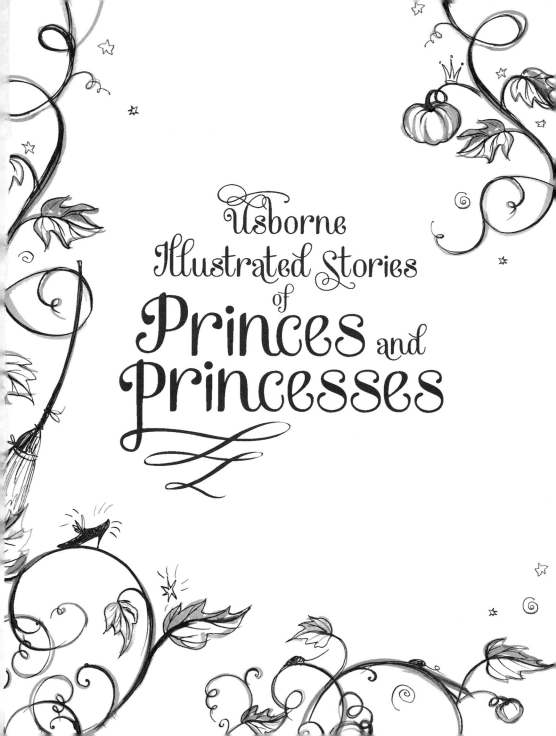

Usborne Illustrated Stories of Princes and Princesses

Usborne Illustrated Stories of Princes and Princesses

Retold by Susanna Davidson,
Rosie Dickins and Anna Milbourne

Illustrated by Alessandra Roberti
Additional illustrations by Antonia Miller

CONTENTS

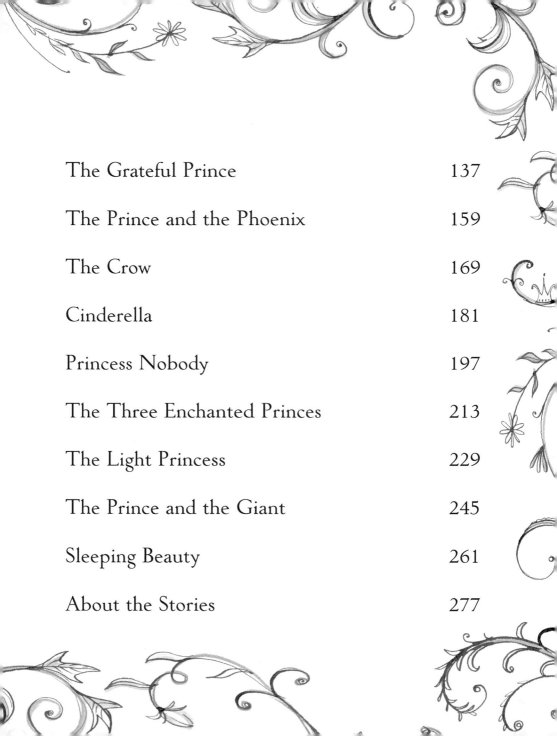

THE FROG PRINCE

Long ago, in a sunny palace garden, a princess was playing with her precious golden ball. She tossed it into the air and caught it over and over again, each time throwing the ball a little higher. The ball whirled and flashed in the sunshine, falling neatly back into her outstretched hands.

But then she threw it a little too far. The golden ball sailed straight over her hands and landed with a "Plop!" in the pond. The princess rushed over just as it sank from view in the murky water.

"It's gone forever," she sobbed, flinging herself down on the grass.

"Whatever is the matter?" asked a croaky little voice.

The princess looked up to see a small, green frog sitting on a lily pad. "What good will it do telling you?" she wailed, rather rudely. "I've lost my golden ball. It's sunk in the water and I'll never get it back."

"You can dry your eyes," the frog said. "I can get your ball back. But what will you give me if I do?"

"Pearls, jewels, my crown, anything!" said the princess. "What do you want?"

"None of those things," replied the frog. "What I want is to eat from your plate and sleep on your pillow, and for you to be my friend."

The princess stared at the green, slimy creature. "What on Earth is it talking about?" she thought. "A frog belongs in a pond, not a palace." But out loud, she said, "Just get the ball back and I promise you can have what you like."

With a wide grin, the frog dived into the pond. The very next moment, it popped back up carrying the golden ball. It swam to the bank and gave the ball to the princess.

"My ball!" she cried happily. Without so much

as a thank you, she ran off
back to the palace.

"Wait for me!" the frog
called after her. But the
princess was already gone.

Later, the princess was sitting at the dinner
table with her mother and father when she heard
a nasty sort of squishy sound. It was coming up
the marble steps outside. Split... splat... split...
splat... then there was a tap at the door.

"Princess, let me in," said a quavery voice.

The princess went to the door and opened it.
To her horror, the frog was sitting on the doorstep.
She slammed the door and ran back to the table.

"Who was it?" asked her father.

Staring down at her soup, her heart pounding,
the princess said, "A revolting frog. It rescued my

golden ball from the pond this afternoon. In return it asked to eat from my plate, sleep on my pillow and be my friend."

"What did you reply?" asked her father.

"I said yes," the princess answered. "But I didn't think I really would have to," she added indignantly. "It's a *frog!*"

"A promise is a promise," said her father. "Let that frog in at once."

Dragging her feet, the princess went and opened the door to the frog. It followed her all the way back to her seat with a hop-split... hop-splat. She sat back down in her chair.

"Princess, please can you lift me up?" croaked the frog from down below.

The princess glowered at her father, who looked back at her sternly. "Go on," he said.

So the princess picked up the frog and put it on the table.

"Thank you, Princess," it croaked and began to share her dinner. It slurped her soup, chomped on her roast potatoes and licked her ice cream. "My compliments to the chef," it told the king and queen politely. "This really is delicious. Aren't you hungry?" it asked the princess.

She shook her head. She felt quite sick just watching it.

"I'm rather sleepy now, can we go to bed?" the frog asked when dinner was over.

At the thought of the clammy, horrible frog sleeping on her lovely silk pillow, the princess let out a moan. "You can't expect me to take it to bed," she groaned at her father.

"A princess always keeps her promises," said her father. "Stop being ungracious and get on with it."

The princess shuddered. She picked up the frog between her finger and her thumb, wrinkling her nose with disgust, and took it to her bedroom. She was about to drop it in a corner, when the frog piped up. "You promised I could sleep on your pillow. Princesses should keep their promises. Your father said as much."

"Oh why won't you just leave me alone?"

burst out the princess, and she flung the frog across the room. It hit the wall with a squelch and slid to the floor.

The princess stared at it for a moment but it didn't move. "Oh no, what have I done?" she whispered in horror. She ran over to the limp frog.

Cradling it in her hands, she lifted the creature up. It looked so helpless and small that she felt sorrier than she had ever felt in her life. "I wish you were still alive," she whispered. She laid the frog gently on her pillow and gave it a little kiss.

She didn't quite know what happened next, but all of a sudden, the thing lying on her pillow wasn't a frog but a prince, and a handsome one at that. He looked at her with friendly eyes and a warm smile, and said, "Thank you once again, kind Princess."

"But what happened to the frog?" she gasped.

"That was me," the prince smiled. "A witch turned me into a frog when I refused to marry her daughter," he explained. "The only thing that could free me was if someone took me, an ugly little creature, into their heart. And you did!"

"Only after throwing you against a wall," the princess said shamefacedly.

"We did get off to a bit of a bad start," the prince admitted. "But I hope we'll have lots of time to make up for it."

The princess laughed. "I hope so too!"

Indeed they did have time to make up for it, for the prince and the princess spent the rest of their days together. And the princess was never, ever cruel to a frog again.

THE MOONLIGHT PRINCESS

Long, long ago in Japan, there lived an old bamboo cutter. He was poor and he was sad, for he and his wife had never had a child of their own. Every morning, he left his house and went into the woods, searching for the spot where the plumes of bamboo waved their feathery leaves against the sky.

He would cut down the bamboo canes and carry them home, where he and his wife would carve furniture from the wood, and make a little money by selling it at market.

One morning, as he set to work cutting down a clump of bamboo, the woods were suddenly flooded with a bright soft light, as if the full moon had just risen. Looking up in astonishment, the old man saw that the brilliant light was streaming from just one bamboo stem. Filled with wonder, he dropped his knife and went towards the light. There, in the green hollow of the stem, was a tiny girl, only three inches high.

Her face was more beautiful than any earthly being.

"We have always longed for a child," thought the old man. "Perhaps this one has been sent to us from the heavens, as our very own." He cradled the girl in his hands and carried her back to his wife.

The old man and his wife were happy from that moment on. All their love was given to the little child. And from time to time, the old man found nuggets of gold, tucked away in the notches of the bamboo in the forest around their home. When he hewed down the bamboo stems and split them open, he found them stuffed with precious stones. Soon, the old couple were rich beyond their dreams.

After three months, the bamboo child had

miraculously become a full-grown girl. As tall now
as any adult, she still looked as if she were made
of light. She filled the house with her moonlit
glow, even in the dark of night.

The old man and his wife tied up her hair and
dressed her in beautiful kimonos.

"She is not of this world,"
they whispered to each
other. And they placed
her behind screens like
a Japanese princess.

When it came to the
naming of their new-found
child, the old couple called in
a celebrated name-giver, and he gave her the
name of Princess Moonlight. "Her body gives out
so much light," he said, "she might have been the

daughter of the Moon God."

Everyone who came to the naming ceremony declared they had never seen anyone so lovely, and the fame of her beauty spread far and wide. Suitors from across the land came to the house, in the hope of winning her hand. But the old man sent them away, for the princess declared she had no desire to marry. So the men made little holes in the fence, in the hope of catching a glimpse of the Moonlight Princess.

Some wearied and went home, but five princes were determined to make her their own. They stood outside, in the burning sun and in floods of rain. Sometimes they wrote letters to the princess, but no answer came back. They waited all winter, through frost and snow, through the gentle warmth of spring and into summer.

At last, the bamboo cutter came out to speak
to them.

"Tell the princess of the gentleness of our
love," they begged. "Tell her how long we have
waited, sleepless and roofless, without food or rest,
in the hope of winning her."

The old man took pity on the faithful suitors.
"What will you do when your mother and I are
dead and gone?" he said to the Moonlight
Princess. "At least consider these five princes. See
if there is one among them you could choose. Will
you refuse to do as I wish?"

"There is nothing I wouldn't do for you,"
replied the Moonlight Princess. "But I must test
their love further before I can agree to speak
to them."

That night, the bamboo cutter went out to

meet the five princes and to tell them of the test. The first prince's quest was to find the stone bowl belonging to the Buddha in India.

The second prince was to go to the Mountain of Horai in the Eastern Sea. From there, he had to bring back a gold and silver branch from the tree that grows on its summit, which bears white jewels on its tips.

The third prince was to go to China and search for the fire-rat and bring her its skin.

The fourth prince was told to search for the dragon that bore the rainbow stone.

And the fifth prince was to find the cowrie shell born from a swallow.

Now, the first prince was afraid to go all the way to India. Instead, he went to a nearby temple and took a stone bowl from the altar. He then wrapped it in a cloth of gold and waited quietly for three years before bringing it to the old man.

When the princess unwrapped the bowl she waited for it to make the room shine with light. When it failed to shine at all, she knew it for a trick, and refused to see the prince. He returned home, having lost all hope of winning the princess.

The second prince left home for Mount Horai, but everyone he met told him the place was only a fable. So he shut himself away on an island, with six skilled goldsmiths, to make a gold and silver branch bearing white jewels for fruit.

When at last it was finished he brought it to the old man who gave it to the princess, who sighed and said that this gift, too, was a fake.

The third prince had a friend in China, so he wrote asking for the skin of the fire-rat, promising any amount of money for it. When at last he received it, he put it carefully in a box and sent it to the princess. She put the skin to the test by lighting a fire, and placing the skin in the bluest, hottest part of the flame, where it crackled and burned at once. She knew, then, that the third prince had also failed in his quest.

The fourth never intended to search for the dragon. He sent his servants instead. They treated the request as a chance for time away, while the prince, thinking he could not fail, prepared his house for the princess. A year passed in waiting, and still his men did not return with the rainbow stone. So the prince was forced to set out on the quest himself. He set sail in his ship, but a great storm blew him far out to sea. After many months, weary and anxious, he felt his love for the princess turn to anger. He decided never to go near her again.

The fifth prince failed even sooner than the rest. As soon as he heard the news of his task, he decided it was impossible. He went home and put the princess out of his mind.

By this time, the fame of Princess Moonlight's beauty had reached the ears of the Emperor himself. He came to the house and immediately fell deeply in love.

"Come to Court," he begged her.

"I cannot," she replied. "I would turn into a shadow." And even as she spoke she began to lose her form.

"I'll promise to leave you free then," said the Emperor. He said goodbye, for it was time for him to return to the Royal Palace. But he left with a sad heart, and spent much of his time writing poems, telling the princess of his love and devotion.

After the Emperor left, the old man noticed the princess began to spend her nights sitting on her balcony, gazing at the Moon. One night the old man found her weeping as if her heart were broken. "What's wrong?" he asked her.

"I don't belong to this world," she confessed. "I come from the Moon and my time on Earth will soon be over. Ten nights from now, my people will come for me, but I have forgotten the Moon-world where I once belonged. I'm weeping to think of leaving the home where I've been so happy for so long."

The old man and his wife were distraught at the thought of losing their foster daughter. So they wrote to the Emperor, to see if there was anything he could do. In reply, he sent two thousand brave warriors to protect the princess. On the tenth night, one thousand stood guard on the roof; another thousand kept watch around the house. The old man gave orders that no one was to sleep. Everyone in the

house had to be ready to fight for the princess.

"Even the Emperor will be powerless against my people," said the princess. "If I could do as I would like, I'd stay with you through your old age, in gratitude for the love and kindness you have shown me all my earthly life."

The night wore on. The yellow harvest Moon rose high, flooding the world with golden light. The bamboo and the pine forests lay silent. At the first light of dawn, all hoped the danger had passed. Suddenly the watchers saw a cloud billowing out from around the Moon, and as they looked, the cloud began to roll towards the Earth. In the middle of the cloud stood a flying chariot, and in the chariot was a band of luminous beings.

One stepped out. He looked like a king, and, poised in the air, he called for the old man to

come out.

"Thank you for taking care of the Moon-child," he said. "We sent her down to you for protection, while we waged celestial war. In return for her safety, we sent you wealth. We put gold and jewels in the bamboo for you to find. But the war is over and the time has come for her to return. Now, Princess Moonlight, come out from the house."

At his words, the screens of her room slid open, and there stood the princess, shining and radiant.

The king led her out and placed her in the chariot. She looked back and called out to the old man and the old woman. "I don't want to leave you. If I could stay, I would. Think of me when you look at the Moon." Then she took off her shawl and gave it to them. "Here is something to remember me by," she said.

One of the Moon-beings in the chariot held up a coat of wings and a phial, full of the Elixir of Life. The princess swallowed a little and tried to give the rest to the old man and his wife, but another Moon-being stepped in front of her and stopped her.

Just before the robe of wings was placed on her shoulders, the Moonlight Princess held up her hands. "Wait!" she said. "I must not forget the Emperor. I must write to him to say goodbye."

She placed the phial of the Elixir of Life in the letter, and asked the old man to give it to the Emperor.

A moment later, the chariot began to roll towards the Moon. As the old man and his wife gazed after the princess, the dawn broke, and in the light of day, the Moon-chariot was lost among the clouds.

Princess Moonlight's letter was taken to the palace. The Emperor was too afraid to touch the Elixir of Life, so he sent it to the top of the most sacred mountain in the land, Mount Fuji. There, it was burned on the summit at sunrise. And to this day, there is smoke rising from the top of Mount Fuji to the clouds above.

THE SEVEN RAVENS

Far away and long ago, there lived a king and queen with seven sons — seven strong, handsome boys, with hair as black as ravens' wings. Their eighth child was a girl, raven-haired like her brothers. But, unlike her brothers, she was born sickly and small.

One morning, when the queen stroked the baby's face, it burned to the touch.

"She has a fever," said the king. "We need cold water to cool her down."

"We'll get some," offered the oldest prince. His six brothers nodded, eager to help. "Water from the spring will be the coldest."

The princes took a jug and dashed off. The path was narrow, and twisted between trees, so they were almost at the spring before they saw an old man. They didn't know it, but he was an enchanter, and a very bad-tempered one at that.

As they squeezed past, one of the princes accidentally stepped on the man's toes.

"Ow!" howled the man furiously. "You clumsy clods, why don't you look where you're putting those big feet of yours?"

His mouth twisted in a sour smile. "Perhaps you should try flying instead." He pointed a long, bony finger. At once, all seven princes began to sprout long, black feathers. Their noses curved and hardened into beaks, while their feet shrank into claws... A moment later, instead of seven princes, there were seven glossy black ravens with bright, startled eyes.

"Now be gone!" snapped the enchanter. There was a flapping and fluttering as seven pairs of wings beat the air... and then silence.

Back in the palace, the king and queen waited in vain for their sons to return. No one had seen what had happened and no trace of the boys could be found. Their only consolation was the little princess, who quickly recovered. With each passing day she grew stronger and more lovely, with raven hair and rose-red lips.

The king and queen never told her how her brothers had disappeared, for fear she might feel somehow to blame. But one day, she overheard two servants gossiping about it — and then she could not rest.

"My brothers vanished trying to help me," she thought to herself. "Now I must help them! I will find them and bring them home."

The princess packed up a loaf of bread, a jug of water and a little wooden chair. On her finger, she placed a golden ring that had been her mother's. And then she set out.

She walked and walked, until her legs ached and her shoes were almost worn through. When she was hungry, she nibbled a crumb of bread. When she was thirsty, she took a sip of water. And when she felt tired or sad, she sat on the chair, held the ring and thought of home.

After many, many days, she came to the wild lands at the end of the world. All around were rocks and thorn bushes. But of her brothers, there was no sign.

"I won't give up," she thought. "Perhaps the sun knows where they are? It sees everything."

She began to walk towards the sun, but it
blazed down at her so fiercely that her face
began to burn and she had to turn away.

"I'll ask the moon instead," she told
herself. But the moon frowned on her so
coldly that her fingers began to turn blue.

She was almost in despair when she heard a
distant whispering. "Come to us," called a hundred
faint, silvery voices. "We can help you." The stars
were speaking to her.

She followed the noise and found the stars,
each sitting and sparkling on its own little chair.
She sat down on her chair and rested while the
morning star, which was the brightest, spoke.

"An enchanter turned your brothers into
ravens and banished them to live inside the glass
mountain. But you can rescue them if you are

brave. The mountain is tall and treacherous, and you will need a key of bone to enter."

The princess felt something in her hand. She looked down and saw a chicken bone.

"Oh thank you," she cried, taking the bone and tucking it carefully into her pocket.

The way to the glass mountain lay through gloomy ravines and dark forests — but the princess went on with a light heart, now she knew she was on the right path.

At last she came to the mountain. Its jagged, glassy slopes glittered like diamonds, rising up steeply to a high, distant peak.

The princess reached out and touched a gleaming ridge. It was as sharp as a knife. She swallowed hard. "If I fall, I shall be cut to pieces..."

Slowly, carefully, she began to climb. The glass was icy cold and horribly slippery. Sometimes it groaned and cracked under her weight. Once or twice, she held her breath as a piece broke away and tumbled down the mountainside to shatter far below.

Just beneath the summit, she came to a door. "This must be it!" she exclaimed. She reached into her pocket to pull out the bone... but her fingers were so stiff and tired, she couldn't hold onto it. "*Nooo!*" The bone fell through the air, bounced once, twice, and broke into splinters.

"Now what shall I do?" she thought, gazing sadly down at her hands. Her fingers were so thin, you could see the bones beneath the skin – for she had finished her bread and water long ago, and there had been nothing to eat since.

"I wonder..."

She stretched out her little finger and tried it in the keyhole... *click!* The door swung open.

Now she found herself in a sparkling cave, high above the world. It was so bright, she had to blink. A shape stirred in the glitter. As it came closer, the princess saw it was a little man with a kind smile.

"What are you looking for, child?" he asked, with a deep bow.

"My brothers, the ravens," said the princess.

The little man nodded. "My lord ravens are not at home," he said. "But you may wait here until they come." And he led her to a table set with seven silver plates and seven golden goblets.

The princess was very hungry and thirsty. So she took one bite from each plate, and one sip from each goblet. As she put down the last goblet, her mother's ring slipped from her thin finger.

Splash! The ring fell into the drink. But the princess didn't notice because, just then, there was another, louder noise. A rushing and whirring...

"Like wings," she thought, her heart racing.

"My lord ravens have come home," announced the man, going to the door.

Feeling suddenly shy, the princess stepped back into the shadows.

One by one, each raven flew in to take its place at the table. "Who has been eating from my plate?" croaked one.

"Who has drunk from my goblet?" cawed another. "Is there a thief among us?"

But the oldest and wisest of the ravens looked all around the cave with twinkling eyes and shook its black feathered head. Then it knocked over its goblet, so the golden ring spilled out and rolled across the table.

"It is our sister the princess, come to set us free," he cried. "Welcome, sister! Come out and join us."

The princess stepped from her hiding place, her hand stretched out in greeting. As she touched each bird, it was transformed into a raven-haired prince, until she was surrounded by her seven long-lost brothers.

Then there was much hugging and talking and delight, and even more when they returned to the king and queen. And they all lived happily together for the rest of their days.

THE TWELVE DANCING PRINCESSES

Once upon a time, there was a king with twelve daughters, each more beautiful than the last. Every night they went quietly to bed, for the king never allowed them to stay up late.

So imagine his surprise when, one morning, the princesses came down to breakfast with tired eyes and their little silk slippers in tatters, as if they had danced the night away.

"What's this?" he demanded. "Where have you been?"

The princesses yawned and rubbed their eyes, and refused to say.

The next night, the king locked their bedroom door. But by morning, the princesses had worn out a second set of slippers. The night after that, the king locked the door *and* put guards around it. But the same thing happened.

In despair, the king issued a royal decree. "If any man can discover where the princesses are going at night, he shall have half my kingdom and the hand of one of the princesses in marriage!"

As word spread, many men took up the challenge, but none succeeded. The king grew grumpier and grumpier. And then a young man carrying a faded, weather-stained cloak arrived.

"My name is Rafe and I'm here for the challenge," he announced.

The king frowned. "I don't want another time-waster," he snapped. "If you fail, I'll throw you in the dungeons!"

Rafe gave a carefree smile. "I don't plan to fail," he replied simply. He caught the eye of Rose, the youngest princess, and winked, making her blush prettily.

"He's too handsome to be locked up," she sighed to her sisters.

"Don't be silly," Amaryllis, the eldest, hissed back. "He *mustn't* find out where we go, or we won't be able to dance any more! Father hates dancing. He never holds any balls."

Rose hung her head. "But still it *is* a shame," she thought.

That night, Rafe took up watch outside the bedroom. Inside, the princesses were chattering and laughing and getting ready for bed. Then the door creaked open and Amaryllis looked out.

"It will be very cold sitting out in the corridor all night," she said kindly. "Won't you have a hot drink?" She passed him a steaming goblet and watched as he lifted it to his lips.

"Mmm, delicious," he sighed. "Thank you."

Amaryllis smiled and closed the door.

As soon as the lock clicked, Rafe emptied the goblet out of a window. "I'm sure that was a sleeping potion," he thought. "I'd better look as if I'm asleep." He sat down on the floor, closed his eyes and began to snore gently.

The door creaked again and Amaryllis peered out at Rafe. "All clear!" she called, ducking back inside. There was a flurry of footsteps, a creak of hinges and then silence.

Rafe opened his eyes. "Time to see what's really going on," he thought. He pulled out his cloak, threw it across his shoulders — and vanished! It was a magic cloak that made the wearer invisible. Quickly, he tiptoed into the princesses' room. "Empty... but what's that?" Underneath a rumpled rug, a secret trap door led down steep steps, into a winding passage.

Rafe ran silently down the steps. He soon caught up with the princesses, beautifully dressed in long silk dresses and sleek new slippers. In his haste, he stepped on the hem of Rose's skirt. "Oh!" she exclaimed. "Someone pulled my dress."

"There's no one there, silly," laughed Amaryllis. "It must have caught on a nail."

The passage ended in an underground forest, where golden leaves rustled on silver branches. Between the leaves, heavy-looking fruit glittered strangely... "Jewels!" realized Rafe, gazing at huge diamonds, sapphires and rubies. When no one was looking, he reached out a hand. *Snap!* He broke off a small branch sparkling with diamonds and tucked it under his cloak.

"Did you hear that?" said Rose. "Someone *is* following us!"

"Don't be silly," sighed Amaryllis. "You must have stepped on a twig."

Beyond the forest lay a glassy lake, lit by strings of silver lanterns. And on an island in the middle stood a castle, its windows glowing invitingly. Lilting music echoed across the water.

A row of boats lined the shore, each with a handsome prince at the oars, ready to row the princesses across. Rafe watched as the princesses boarded, then stepped quickly after Rose.

"This boat feels heavier than usual," she said, with a frown.

"Because you ate too much dinner," called over Amaryllis, from her boat. "Now stop worrying!"

Before Rose could answer, they were there.

The princes and princesses stepped out of the boats and swept up the steps in a swish of silks. Rafe darted after them.

Now they were in a magnificent ballroom, lined with gleaming mirrors and lit by golden candlelight. Rafe couldn't see any musicians but somehow music filled the air. The princes bowed to the princesses, took their hands and began to waltz. They danced for hours, never pausing or growing tired, swirling and twirling gracefully in time to the never-ending music.

"This is truly an enchanted place," thought Rafe, watching. "Although nothing here is as enchanting as Rose..."

At last, a clock chimed. The sisters shook themselves, as if waking from a dream.

"Time to go," called Amaryllis.

The princesses hurried home, their dancing shoes in tatters once again. Rafe was close behind. Back in their room, they climbed yawning into bed, while he pulled off his cloak and sat down outside the door as if he'd never been away.

In the morning, the king summoned Rafe to his throne room. "Well?" he said curtly. Behind the throne, Rose held her breath.

Rafe smiled. "Your Majesty, your daughters have been dancing in an enchanted castle, deep under the ground."

The king snorted with laughter. "Don't be ridiculous..." he began. But he stopped abruptly when Rafe held up the branch of diamonds.

"Where did you get that?" he demanded.

So Rafe told him about the secret trap door, and how he had followed the princesses through the underground forest to the castle by the lake.

When he had finished, the king nodded slowly. "I can see you are telling the truth. You have succeeded in the challenge. Half my kingdom is yours! Which of my daughters would you like to marry?"

In reply, Rafe sank down onto one knee. "Princess Rose," he said, gazing shyly up at her. "If she will have me?"

"Oh yes," said Rose, blushing happily.

"I suppose now there will be no more dancing," sighed Amaryllis.

"Oh but there will," insisted Rafe. "I love dancing and I promise to hold plenty of balls!" And he did.

THE FLOWER QUEEN'S DAUGHTER

The young prince galloped across the meadow, his mare's hooves thudding deep into the damp earth, gouging up great clods of dirt. Then, without warning, the mare gave a snort and reared up. The prince clung on, as his horse's hooves flailed over an open ditch.

The prince cried out, yanking at the reins and turning the mare aside, when he heard, "Help me! Help me!" Looking down, he saw an old woman, cowering in the bottom of the ditch.

"Please help, I'm stuck in here," she said.

The prince jumped down and reached out his hands. "What happened to you?" he asked, as he pulled the old woman out.

"I was selling eggs in town," replied the old woman. "But I lost my way in the dark and fell into this deep ditch. I might have been here forever if you hadn't rescued me."

"Come," said the prince. "I will put you on my horse and lead you home. Where do you live?"

"Over there, at the edge of the forest," said the woman, pointing to a little hut in the distance.

The prince lifted her onto his horse and they

set off, the old woman murmuring her thanks all the while. When they reached the hut, the old woman took the prince by the hand. "You are mighty," she said, "but you also have a kind heart, which deserves to be rewarded. Would you like to have the most beautiful woman in the world as your wife?"

"Oh yes!" replied the prince. "But how could I hope to find her?"

"The most beautiful woman in the world is the daughter of the Queen of the Flowers. She has been captured by a dragon. If you wish to marry her, you must first set her free. Take this little bell," she added, drawing one out from her pocket. "Ring it once and the King of the Eagles will come. Ring it twice and the King of the Foxes will appear. Ring it three times and you will see the

King of the Fishes."

She handed him the little bell and with a small 'ting' she disappeared, hut and all, as if the earth had swallowed her up.

"I must have been speaking to a fairy..." the prince thought. He put the little bell in his pocket and rode home, amazed by what had happened; eager to begin his quest.

For a year, the prince roamed the world. But he found no trace of dragons, or word of the Flower Queen's daughter. Then, one summer's day as the dusk drew in, he met a very old man, sitting in front of a hut. "Do you know where the daughter of the Flower Queen is kept prisoner?" he asked.

"No I do not," replied the old man. "But if you go along this road for a year, you will reach the hut where my father lives. He may be able to tell you."

The prince thanked him and carried on his journey for another year along the same road. At the end of it, he came to a hut where he found an even older man. He asked the same question, and the man answered, "No, I do not. But go straight along this road for another year and you will come to the hut where my father lives. I know he can help you."

So the prince wandered on for another year, always on the same road, and at last reached the hut where he found the third old man.

"Ah!" said the old man, in answer to the question. "The dragon lives up there on the mountain, and he has just begun his year of sleep. But if you want to see the Flower Queen's daughter, go to the mountain beyond. The dragon's old mother lives there. She has balls every night and the Flower Queen's daughter often goes along to dance."

So the prince climbed up the mountain beyond and found a castle made of gold, set with diamond windows. He pushed open the front gate and seven dragons rushed at him.

"What do you want?" they asked, their fiery breath tickling his neck.

"I would like to see the Mother Dragon," the prince replied, undaunted. "I've heard so much of her beauty and kindness."

The seven dragons nodded, smiling, pleased with the prince's flattery. "Come with me," said the eldest, "and I will take you to her."

The dragon led the prince through room after

room, each more splendid than the last. In the twelfth room they found the Mother Dragon, sitting on a jewel-covered throne. She had three heads, covered in gleaming green scales. Her voice was like the croaking of ravens.

"Why have you come here?" she demanded.

"I have heard of your beauty and your kindness," lied the prince. "And I would like to enter your service."

"Very well," rasped the Mother Dragon. "But first you must lead my mare out to the meadow and look after her for three days. If you don't bring her home safely each evening, we will eat you."

She smiled broadly, showing rows of flashing

teeth. The prince bowed low to hide his fear. "Take me to your mare," he said.

But no sooner had the prince led the mare to the meadow, than she vanished. The prince searched everywhere for her, and at last sat down in despair. A shadow passed over him. He looked up and saw an eagle, soaring overhead.

"The bell!" he remembered. Taking it out of his pocket, he rang it once. In a moment, he heard a rustling in the air, followed by a swooshing of wide wings – and the King of the Eagles landed at his feet.

"I know what you want," said the King of the Eagles. "You are looking for the Mother Dragon's mare, which is galloping among the clouds. I will summon all the eagles of the air. We will catch the mare and bring her to you."

So saying, the King of the Eagles flew away. The prince waited out in the meadow, and as dusk drew in he heard a mighty rushing sound and felt the wind in his hair. When he looked up he saw thousands of eagles driving the mare before them. He caught the mare by her mane, swung himself onto her back and rode straight to the Mother Dragon.

"You have succeeded in your task for the day," she said. "As your reward, you may come to my ball tonight."

She gave him a copper cloak and led him to a grand ballroom, where he-dragons and she-dragons danced together. The Flower Queen's daughter stood in their midst. Her cheeks bloomed like roses, her skin was as fair as lilies and her dress was woven from flowers. The prince asked her to dance, and as they whirled across the floor, he whispered in her ear, "I have come to set you free!"

She smiled. "If you bring the mare back on the third day, ask the Mother Dragon to give you the mare's foal as your reward."

Early the next morning, the prince led the Mother Dragon's mare out into the meadow. As before, she vanished before his eyes, so he took out his little bell and rang it twice.

In a moment, the King of the Foxes stood before him. "I already know what you want," he said. "I will summon all the foxes of the world to find the mare who has hidden herself on the hill."

With these words, the King of the Foxes disappeared, and in the evening thousands of foxes brought the mare back to the prince.

This time, the Mother Dragon rewarded the prince with a silver cloak and a second invitation to her ball.

The Flower Queen's daughter smiled to see him safely back. When they danced, she whispered in his ear, "If you succeed again tomorrow, wait for me with the foal in the meadow. Then after the ball, we will ride away together."

On the third day, the prince led the mare to the meadow and saw her vanish before his eyes. This time, he took out the little bell and rang it three times.

In a moment, the King of the Fishes appeared

before him. "I know what you want me to do," he said. "I will summon all the fishes of the sea and tell them to bring back the mare who is hiding in the river."

Just before evening, the mare burst out of the river from a riot of flashing fins. The prince grabbed hold of her mane and rode her home to the Mother Dragon.

"You are brave," she said. "You deserve a place in my service. But first, I shall give you a reward."

Remembering the words of the Flower Queen's daughter, the prince begged for a foal from her mare. And the Mother Dragon gave it to him, along with a cloak made of gold.

That evening, the prince appeared at the ball in his golden cloak, but before the clock struck midnight, he slipped away. He went straight to the stables, where he mounted his foal and rode out into the meadow to wait for the Flower Queen's daughter. When she came, shining like the moon, her scent as sweet as jasmine, she swung herself up in front of him on the foal. Then they flew like the wind until they reached the Flower Queen's palace.

But the Mother Dragon's sons had seen them go and they woke their sleeping brother.

"How dare she escape?" he snorted, breathing fumes of rage. He flapped his leathery wings until he came to the Flower Queen's palace.

There, he lashed out great tongues of flame, but the Flower Queen was ready with her magic. His fire turned into a forest of flowers, as high as the sky, and there was nothing he could do to get past it.

When the Flower Queen heard her daughter wanted to marry the prince, she consented gladly. They were married the next day, and lived happily together in the palace, deep in the forest of flowers.

RHODOPSIS
AND THE
ROSE-RED
SLIPPERS

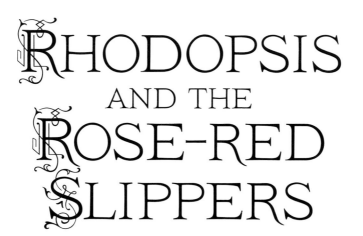

Long, long ago, when pharaohs were still the kings of Egypt, there lived a beautiful young girl named Rhodopsis. She had been born in a far-off land, and brought to Egypt by pirates. Now she worked as a servant for a wealthy merchant.

The merchant was a good man, but he was old and spent much of the day sleeping. And while he slept, his other servants taunted Rhodopsis. She looked very different from them, and they hated her for it. They would pull her soft, fair hair and send her out to work in the midday sun, until the heat made her pale face blush a rosy red. Then they would laugh and toss their dark braids, turn up their dusky faces scornfully and call her 'Rosy-cheeks'.

But the merchant treated Rhodopsis with kindness. He loved her unusual looks and the stories she could tell — fascinating tales of animals and birds and people from her homeland. Often, he gave her gifts, a dish of sweet, sticky dates or a string of turquoise beads. Once, observing how her feet were too small for the rough straw sandals she wore, he brought her a pair of slippers made of soft rose-red leather, decorated with delicate golden patterns.

"Oh thank you," cried Rhodopsis, trying one on her tiny foot. It was just the right size.

The other servants watched jealously. "Why should *she* get fancy shoes?" sneered one.

"They look ridiculous," jeered another. "Far too fine for a servant girl! We'd better make sure she doesn't forget her place."

As soon as the merchant fell asleep, they sent Rhodopsis down to the river with a big basket of dirty linen. "Make sure you wash it well and rinse it three times," they snapped.

Rhodopsis set off obediently, lugging the heavy basket. The sun blazed down, making her cheeks flush as she followed the dusty track. It wound past rustling palm trees, down through lush green fields to the river.

As she approached, little birds darted away with fluttering wings. Somewhere in the distance, she heard the low bellow of hippos. The riverbank was muddy and thick with reeds. Further out, blue water glittered fiercely in the bright sunlight.

"I'll have to wade all the way in to do the washing," Rhodopsis realized. She took off her slippers and left them on a rock, then stepped into the water. It felt deliciously cool.

Suddenly, a dark shadow skimmed across the water. One of the birds gave a shrill alarm call. Rhodopsis glanced up and saw a falcon diving out of the sky, curved wings gleaming, talons out... Before she could move, it was soaring up into the air again, clutching a rose-red slipper.

"Oh no!" Rhodopsis splashed back to the bank, snatched up the other slipper and put it safely in her pocket. "I hope the merchant won't be angry." She watched, sadly, as the falcon disappeared into the distance.

Straight as an arrow, the falcon flew to the city of Memphis, to the pharaoh's great white palace by the River Nile. It hovered high above the rooftops, then suddenly swooped low over a courtyard where the pharaoh and his family were sitting on soft cushions, and dropped the slipper into the lap of his eldest son.

They all glanced up in astonishment. When the pharaoh saw the bird, he gasped. "The falcon is a sacred bird. This is a sign from the gods!"

The prince studied the slipper curiously. "It's so small and delicate... I don't know who it belongs to, but I must find her."

The pharaoh nodded his agreement. "Bring the royal barge!"

So the prince set sail in a canopied barge, following the broad blue Nile, past fragrant lotus blossoms and waving reeds. In every town, his messengers went ashore to make an announcement:

"Whoever fits this rose-red slipper, the pharaoh's son desires to meet her."

Then the women would crowd around to admire the fine red shoe, hoping to claim it was theirs, but it was always too small for them.

Eventually the barge came to the town where the merchant lived. As word of its arrival spread, a crowd gathered. With a loud fanfare, two haughty-looking messengers stepped ashore.

The people at the front of the crowd bowed so low, their noses touched the ground. Rhodopsis hid shyly near the back. But, when she heard the messengers' announcement, she came timidly out. With blushing cheeks, she slid a tiny foot into the rose-red slipper. It was a perfect fit.

"Thank you for bringing it back to me," she said softly, pulling the matching slipper out of her pocket and sliding it onto her other foot. The crowd looked at the shoes and cheered.

Then the messengers took her hand and led her onto the barge to meet the prince. As soon as he saw her, he knew she was the one for him. "The gods themselves have brought us together," he told her

86

humbly. "Will you marry me and be my wife?"

Rhodopis met his strong, dark eyes and smiled. "Yes," she said. "With my whole heart."

"But sire," stuttered an advisor. "You can't marry a servant... I mean... she isn't even an Egyptian!"

The prince shook his head. "She is more Egyptian than any of us," he replied. "Her hair is the gold of desert sands, her eyes are as blue as the waters of the Nile, and her smile is as enchanting as the Sphinx that guards the great pyramids. I will marry no one else."

So it was that Rhodopis, the servant girl, married the pharaoh's son. In time, they became the king and queen of Egypt, and ruled wisely and well to the end of their days.

THE PRINCESS ON THE GLASS HILL

Beside the river there was a meadow, and in the meadow there was a barn, built to store hay. But for the past two years the barn had lain empty, for something mysterious was happening every Midsummer's Eve...

Just when the grass stood greenest and deepest, the meadow was eaten down to the ground, so that next morning, it all lay bare. It happened once, it happened twice, until the farmer said to his three sons, "One of you must go and sleep in the barn next Midsummer's Eve, and find out what's been eating my grass."

The eldest son went first to watch the meadow. "You can trust me to look after your grass, Father," he boasted.

When Midsummer's Eve came, he set off to the barn and lay down to sleep. But in the night he heard a great clattering and a battering. The walls of the barn trembled, they creaked and groaned and the earth itself shook. The eldest son jumped up and ran as fast as he could, not looking back until he reached home. And that year, the grass was eaten up, every single last blade, just as it had been twice before.

A year later, and the second son trudged off to the barn, boasting that he would save the grass. But as the night wore on, there was a rumbling and a trembling and a quaking, even worse than the year before, and the second son ran home as fast as he could go.

Next year came the turn of the third son. His brothers called him Boots, as they made him spend his time cleaning theirs. And they laughed at him for loving to sit by the fire, with his feet among the cinders.

"You'll never manage it," scoffed his brothers, as he set off.

"You're only good for toasting yourself by the fire and cleaning up after your elders and betters."

Boots stumped up the hill to the barn, not caring about their taunts. Then he waited for night to come.

The barn began to creak and groan. The ground rumbled and quaked, but Boots sat through it all, even though he thought the roof might come down on his head. Then, when all was still, he heard a noise as if a horse were standing outside, cropping the grass. He crept to the door and peered through a hole between the planks. There stood a horse, feeding, but it was the biggest, fattest, grandest horse Boots had ever seen. It had a saddle and a bridle and by its side, on the grass, lay battle dress for a knight, all made of gleaming brass.

Boots lost no time. He was
out of the door, pulling on the
knight's clothes, then leaping up,
up into the air and onto
the horse's back.
And from the
moment he sat there,
legs astride its great
girth, the horse became so
tame he rode away on it, to a secret place where
no one would find it.

"Well," said Boots, when he got home, "I lay in
the barn until the sun rose and I never saw or
heard anything. I don't know why you two were
so scared."

"Ha!" said the brothers. "We'll soon see how
well you watched the meadow." They set off, but

when they reached the meadow, there stood the grass as thick and deep as the night before.

The next Midsummer's Eve was the same. Boots was the only one who dared to go back to the field. As he lay in the barn, there was a clatter and a quake, followed by another clatter and a quake, only this year the sound was even worse than the year before. Then all at once everything was still, and Boots stole to the door and peered through the hole. And there was another horse, chewing and champing at the grass. It was even finer and fatter than last year's horse, with a saddle on its back and a bridle on its neck, and a shining suit of silver, fit for a knight, by its side.

Once again, Boots flung on the suit and leaped onto the horse's back, while it stood still as a lamb. Then he rode the horse to his hiding place and settled it with the first one. After that he went home.

"I suppose you're going to tell us you succeeded again?" asked his brother.

"Go and see for yourselves!" boasted Boots. His brothers ran off to see, and there stood the grass, as thick and deep as the night before.

When the third Midsummer's Eve came, the elder two still didn't have the courage to lie out in the barn and watch the grass. But Boots dared to go, and the same thing happened, except that the shaking and the quaking, the clattering and the battering were worse than ever. When it was over, Boots crept outside, quivering with shock. There stood a horse — far, far bigger and fatter than the two he had taken before. This one had a golden saddle and bridle that shimmered and shone, and a golden battle dress beside it.

Boots pulled on the knight's clothes, leaped on the horse's back and rode it to the hiding place. But when he got home, his brothers were too busy to mock him, or to go and see the grass, just as thick and deep as twice before. Instead their minds were full of the king's daughter, the princess...

"Her father has put her on the hill of glass, next to the palace, with three golden apples in her lap. All across the land, everyone is saying that the man who can ride up and carry off the three golden apples will be given half the kingdom, and the princess as his wife. We're going to set out to the glass hill today to see who wins the princess."

"I'll come too!" cried Boots.

"Oh no you won't," said his brothers. "Look at you, covered in dirt from cleaning our shoes and shifting the cinders, and your clothes are all crumpled and torn. People will make fun of us if we're seen with you."

They set off without a backwards glance, and when they came to the glass hill, they found knights and princes, all struggling up the slippery slope, riding their horses until they were all in a foam. But it was no good. The hill was too smooth and too steep, and each one rode and slipped, and slipped and rode, until their horses were too weary to lift a leg.

"We give up!" cried the knights and princes.

Then all at once, a knight came riding up on the largest steed anyone had ever seen. He wore a brass suit, and the horse had a brass bit in its mouth, so bright that sunbeams shone from it.

"It's no good," the others called out to him. "You'll never make it up that hill. All of us have tried and all of us have failed."

But the knight took no notice, and rode his horse up the hill as if it were covered in grass. When he was about a third of the way, he turned his horse around and rode down again.

"Oh!" thought the princess. "Such a lovely knight... if only he might come all the way up."

And when she saw him turning back, she threw one of the golden apples from her lap, so that it rolled down to him. He picked up the apple, then rode off so fast that no one could tell what had become of him.

That evening, Boots' brothers came home, with

a long story of the knight who had disappeared.

"He could have easily ridden the whole way up!" they said. "But he turned around and rode back down."

"I wish I could have seen him," said Boots, sitting by the fireside.

The next day, the brothers set off again, to watch the contest on the glass hill.

"Oh! Let me come with you," begged Boots.

"You're too dirty," chanted his brothers. "You'll only embarrass us. Stay sitting in the ashes, where you belong."

When the brothers arrived at the glass hill, the same happened as the day before. The knights and princes rode and slipped, and slipped and rode, but not one could get up the hill. And when they had worn out their horses, a knight came riding on a steed even braver and finer than the last. The horse had a silver saddle and bridle, and the knight wore silver, all shining so brightly that the sunbeams danced over them.

Once again, everyone called out to him, "You can't do it!" But the knight paid no heed to them and rode straight up the hill, until he had gone two-thirds of the way, and then he wheeled his horse around and rode down again.

The princess watched him and wished he would ride to the very top, so when she saw him turning back, she threw him the second apple. But as soon as he caught it, he rode off so fast that no one could follow him.

The brothers went home again, and told Boots all that had happened.

"Oh!" said Boots. "I wish I could have seen him."

The third day, Boots once again begged to go with his brothers, but they wouldn't hear of it.

When the brothers reached the glass hill this time, the knights had already given up, and everyone was waiting for the silver knight. But they neither saw nor heard him. Then, at last, a knight came thundering past in a suit of gold, with a golden saddle and bridle so bright that everyone had to shield their eyes. He rode straight to the hill and tore up it, all the way to the top, where he plucked the third golden apple straight from the princess's lap. Then he turned his horse and rode down again, charging away at full speed.

"What a grand knight," said the brothers, when they got home. "The grandest knight in the world."

"Oh!" said Boots. "I wish I could have seen him."

"Ha!" laughed the brothers. "His battle dress

shone brighter than the glowing coals you are always poking away at. You're not fit to touch the ground he walks on."

The next day, all the knights and princes were to pass before the princess, to see if any of them could bring forth the golden apples. But not one of them could produce them.

"I want every man in the kingdom to come to the palace," declared the king. "Someone must have the golden apples."

All the men came to the king's palace, one after the other, but no one had a golden apple.

At last, it was Boots' brothers' turn, and as they were the final two, the king asked if there was anyone left in the kingdom who hadn't come.

"Oh yes," they said. "We have a brother, but he could never have carried off a golden apple. He just sits in a heap by the fire, with his feet stirring the cinders."

"Never mind that!" said the king. "He must come like all the rest."

So the brothers went back and ordered Boots to go to the palace.

"Well now," said the king. "Have you got a golden apple? Speak out!"

"I have," Boots replied. "Here is the first, here is the second, and here is the third, too." So saying, he pulled the golden apples from his pockets. Then he threw off his sooty rags and stood before them in his gleaming golden suit.

"There you are!" said the king. "You shall have my daughter, and half my kingdom, for you deserve both."

Boots' brothers could only gape and stare.

Boots and the princess were married, and
there was great merry-making at the bridal feast.
And all I can say is, if they haven't ceased their
merry-making, they're celebrating still.

THE UGLY PRINCE

Once upon a long ago, a baby was born to a king and queen. "A prince!" cried the midwife. "A beautiful... oh. Oh dear." Her smile fell a little as she looked at the baby. "Well, a baby boy, anyway." Gently, she placed him in his crib.

The queen peered inside and saw the oddest looking baby lying there. His eyes were scrunched and black and his nose was huge. His arms were skinny, his hands were unusually large and knobbly, and he had a tuft of hair sticking up on his head. She stroked the little tuft gently and said, "We'll call him Tufty."

At Prince Tufty's christening, the king quietly asked the baby's fairy godmother, "For his own sake, can you not make him better looking?"

"Sorry," said the fairy godmother shaking her head, "I can't change his looks. But what I can do is give him this fairy gift: whoever he falls in love with will become as witty and clever as he is."

Around the same time, on the other side of an enormous forest, twin girls had been born to another king and queen. One girl was the most beautiful baby ever seen, and the other was not such a beauty. They were christened Bella and Bettina. "Oh at least one of them is good looking," the queen crowed at their christening.

Their fairy godmother frowned at her. "I'd better even things up a little," she muttered. Peering into the crib at the not-quite-so beautiful Bettina, she said, "You shall have wit and charm, to match the beauty of your sister."

To the beautiful Bella, she said, "And your gift, little one, is this: whoever you fall in love with will become as beautiful as you are."

The girls grew up devoted to one another. But the older they grew, the more unhappy Bella became. "I wish I were more like you," she told her sister. "You're so clever and funny. Everyone wants to talk to you. I even bore myself."

"But Bella, you're so beautiful," Bettina protested, stroking her sister's shining hair. "The only reason people come near me is so they can sit by you. Please don't be sad."

They were both right. People were drawn to Bella's beauty like moths to a flame, but quickly lost interest when they found she had little to say. Bettina, however, grew more and more interesting to people the longer they spent with her. Soon she had friends and admirers a-plenty, whereas beautiful Bella, strangely, had very few.

On the other side of the forest, Prince Tufty had grown up into a charming fellow. His looks were no less strange, but everybody who knew him loved him. He was witty, clever and kind, and said things nobody had thought of saying before. But whenever new visitors came to the palace, which was often, they looked at him with pity rather than admiration. This made him terribly sad, and he took to wandering through the forest to be alone. "No girl will ever love me," he sighed to himself. "I'm far too ugly."

In the forest one afternoon, he came across a beautiful princess. She was sitting by a lake staring at her reflection, but looking more unhappy than he thought possible.

"Excuse me," he said. "What's wrong? I can't bear to see such a beautiful face looking so sad."

The girl looked up, startled. "Beauty's only skin deep," she blurted out. "If a person is boring or stupid, it counts for very little."

Prince Tufty smiled. "Boring, stupid people rarely see themselves as that. I'd go so far as to say that if you call yourself boring and stupid, it cannot be true."

The girl's brow wrinkled in confusion. "You see? I am too stupid to understand what you mean!" she exclaimed. "All I know is I'd rather be as ugly as you than as stupid as me." Her eyes suddenly widened and she flushed with embarrassment. "I'm so sorry – I didn't mean to be so rude," she stammered.

But Prince Tufty was laughing. "No matter," he said. "I find you perfectly lovely."

A radiant smile lit up her face and Prince Tufty almost melted into the forest floor with delight. "What is your name?" he managed to ask.

"Bella," answered Bella. "Perhaps we could be

friends?" she added shyly.

"Friends... yes of course," said the prince.

They strolled in the forest, laughing at squirrels' antics, admiring primroses and listening out for woodpeckers. They found so much to do and to talk about that they didn't notice time slipping by.

When the sunlight started to blaze red through the trees, Bella said, "Goodness, it's late. I have to go."

"Will you meet me here next week?" begged Prince Tufty.

"Yes, I'll be here," said Bella, and she ran off through the forest.

After that, they met in the same place every

week. Spring turned to summer and they were both glad to get away from their stuffy palaces into the cool shade of the trees.

Somehow in the company of the attentive prince, Bella found she had lots to say. She didn't feel dull or boring at all. And, in the warmth of their friendship, the prince forgot about feeling ugly. They were both truly happy.

"I like being with you," said Bella one day. "You make me feel *interesting*. When I go back home, though, I'm just the same: pretty dull."

Prince Tufty turned to her earnestly. "I don't think you're dull and I don't see how anyone else possibly could. I love you."

In that moment, Tufty's fairy godmother's

magic worked its spell, and the princess really did become as witty and clever as Prince Tufty.

"You are my best friend in the whole world," she said to him. "I don't ever want to lose you."

"Then marry me!" cried the prince.

The princess stared at him in surprise. In all their time together, she had never once considered him a possible husband.

The prince's face fell a little. "I forgot myself," he said. "You'd be a laughing stock with me as a husband..."

"You mustn't say such a thing," the princess protested. "It's just I've never thought of us in that way before."

"I'll tell you what. I'll give you some time to think about it," said Prince Tufty gallantly. "A year to the day we first met, you can tell me your

answer. We'll meet by the lake on that very day.
And I won't mention it again until then."

The two parted that afternoon, and Prince
Tufty didn't dare ask Bella if she would meet him
as usual the following week.

That night, Bella's parents were throwing a
dinner party. Usually, Bella hated dinner parties as
she found herself with nothing to say, but this
evening she was bursting with conversation. Her
eyes sparkled and her cheeks glowed as she
chatted with the prince sitting next to her.

She was so happy that she scarcely noticed as one prince after another leaned in to hear what she was saying. Her sister watched contentedly as Bella drew the attention of the whole table.

The next day, everybody was talking about Bella. The princes who had been at the dinner party sighed over their breakfasts for love of her. Invitations flooded in – for parties and balls and to go riding with this or that prince.

Bella was so busy all week that she forgot to go to the forest to meet her friend. And the next week she had visitors, and besides, it was a little chilly to spend an afternoon in the forest... By the following week she supposed, with a pang of regret, that Prince Tufty would have stopped going.

The days grew colder. In the forest, the leaves fell from the trees and the wind ruffled the squirrels' tails as they scurried around trying to hide their stores of nuts. Prince Tufty watched them, wandering through the trees, lost as a windblown leaf without his friend.

Soon the first snow fell. The princess was busy with skating parties and skiing trips, sleigh rides and snug fireside dinners. She had more invitations than she knew what to do with.

One set of lonely footprints was left in the fresh snow in the forest. Only the squirrels and huddled little birds saw the prince pass by.

Christmas came and went. Bella had a mountain of presents from all her new friends, and three proposals of marriage. "Which one will you choose?" her sister Bettina asked her as they lay in their beds on New Year's morning.

"Any of them would make a fine husband," Bella replied. "They are all very handsome." But then she stared out of the window at the treetops beyond the palace walls and fell silent. "I don't want to marry any of them," she said sadly.

"Bella, tell me what's wrong," her sister said. "You used to go out for walks in the forest and come back so cheerful. And now I know you're happy that everybody likes you, but somehow you seem a bit sadder, too."

Bella was surprised. She'd never told her sister once about Prince Tufty. It had been her secret, but that morning she told Bettina everything. "But he isn't handsome and dashing, like a prince is supposed to be," she finished rather lamely.

"Do you think I am any less worthy of your love for not being as beautiful as you?" Bettina asked her. And Bella shook her head.

Soon, the snow began to melt. Birds sang in the trees once more, and buds burst from the twigs. Squirrels chased their tails and danced along the branches above Prince Tufty as he walked in the forest.

One fine morning he called out to them. "Today is the day Bella will come back to me," he said joyfully. "Today is a year since we met. Today I will see her again. Perhaps she will even agree to marry me!"

The squirrels ran on, and told the bluebirds, who twittered to the blackbirds, who twittered to the jays. All the animals were so happy for the

prince that they gathered flowers and strung garlands of them between the trees above the lake. The prince was delighted, and waited there for Bella to come.

At the edge of the forest, Bella was heading out of the palace garden gates. She stopped to look at all the little blossoms and listen to the birdsong. She breathed in the fresh air and sighed with happiness at being in the forest again.

She thought of her friend, waiting for her, and found her footsteps becoming quicker and quicker, until finally she broke into a run.

A trill of birdsong announced her arrival at the lake. "I'm sorry I didn't come and see you for this long," she said breathlessly. "I've missed you so much."

"I'm so happy to see you!" the prince cried, leaping to his feet. "I couldn't be sad about anything now you're here again." He took her hands and beamed from ear to ear. Then he looked a little shy, and said, "Have you given any thought to my proposal...?"

Bella gazed at the prince's gentle face and realized she loved him with all her heart. "Oh you *are* a handsome prince," she cried, "and you are so clever and kind. Nothing would make me happier than to marry you, Prince Tufty."

In that moment, her fairy godmother's words came true and the prince became as handsome as the princess was beautiful. His eyes sparkled warmly and his long nose looked more regal than it had ever done before. Almost as if he felt the transformation, the prince straightened his back and smiled.

The happy couple were married the very next week in the forest where they had met. They lived happily ever after, with a tumble of beautifully carefree children.

You might wonder whether it really was fairy magic that made the princess clever and the prince handsome, or whether it was simply the power of love. Only the fairy godmothers would know. They were at the wedding, but nobody thought to ask them then. Perhaps, if you ever meet them, you could ask them for yourself.

THE PRINCESS AND THE PEA

There was once a prince, who wanted very much to find a princess to marry. In those days, the world was full to the brim with princesses, so the prince decided to travel the world to find the right one for him.

After a year had passed, he returned home with a face as long as his shadow. "I didn't find one," he told his mother and father gloomily.

"You didn't find a single princess?" his father asked in disbelief.

"Oh, there were princesses," said the prince. "Plenty of them: pretty ones, chatty ones, sporty ones, bookish ones, musical ones and exotic ones... But not a single *real* princess," he sniffed.

"Did they all have kings and queens as fathers and mothers?" asked the king.

"Yes," admitted the prince.

"Then how much more real could they be?" asked the king, scratching his beard in confusion.

The queen rolled her eyes. "He means they weren't *right* for him," she said, patting her son's hand. "Still," she turned to her son and smiled, "you can stay with us now. You never have to leave home."

The prince looked at her mournfully. "I'll be in my room until supper," he said.

That evening, the weather took a turn for the worse. Dark clouds rolled in until the sky was heavy and brooding. Lightning flashed and thunder rolled, and great drops of rain started to fall. The rain pittered and pattered, then poured and hammered. Torrents of rainwater rushed off the palace roof and flooded the courtyard. Anyone unlucky enough to get caught in the downpour was soaked to the bone in seconds.

Just before supper, there was a knock at the palace door. The king was passing so he answered it himself. Standing there was a girl about his son's age, who was absolutely drenched.

Her hair hung in soggy rats'
tails around her shoulders and
her dress dripped into her
shoes. "Hello there," she said.
"Sorry to arrive so dreadfully
bedraggled. I heard the
prince was back, and that he's
looking for a princess. I happen
to be looking for a prince, so I
thought I'd come and meet him."

"My dear, you look half drowned. Come in,"
said the king. And he led the princess into the
throne room and introduced her to his wife.

The queen looked the princess up and down
from her soaking-wet hair to her squelchy shoes.
"My son returned from his travels around the
world looking for a real princess, but he says he

hasn't found one," she said pointedly. "Not one in all the *world*."

The princess smiled. "I'm a real princess," she assured the queen.

"We'll see about that," the queen thought. To the princess, she said, "You may join us for supper and stay the night. You can't possibly go home in this weather."

After ordering a dry change of clothes for the princess, the queen excused herself and went to organize a bedroom for their guest. "Bring a dried pea from the kitchen," she told the chambermaids who looked at her agog, and then hurried off to do as they were told.

When they returned, the queen placed the pea in the middle of the princess's bed. "Now bring twenty soft mattresses," she ordered. "And twenty of the softest feather quilts, too," she added.

The mattresses were stacked up in a tower on the bed, with feather quilts between them, and the queen declared the room ready.

She returned downstairs to find her son and the princess deep in conversation. All through supper they talked about everything under the sun. They seemed to understand one another perfectly. The princess was such good company that the king and queen enjoyed themselves too.

Time flew by, and before they knew it, it was bedtime. The queen showed the princess to her room. "What a comfortable looking bed!" the girl exclaimed in surprise when she saw the tower of mattresses. Then she turned to the queen, "However am I to get up there?"

"With a ladder of course," the queen said,

as though it was the most normal way in the world to get into bed. She rang a bell, and two footmen appeared, carrying a very long ladder which they propped up by the side of the bed.

"Well then, goodnight," said the queen. "You'll find a nightgown under your pillow."

"Goodnight," said the princess, and climbed the ladder to bed.

The next morning, the princess came down for breakfast looking rather tired. "How did you sleep?" the queen asked her.

"I don't mean to be rude, as you have been so wonderfully welcoming," said the princess. "But I slept dreadfully. There was something small and hard in the middle of the bed and I just couldn't get comfortable all night long."

"Splendid," the queen beamed.

"Mother!" exclaimed the prince in horror, and the king looked at his wife aghast. "She's finally lost her mind," he thought.

"Don't fuss. It's quite all right," said the queen. "I've just proven that this young lady is, in fact, a real princess." She whispered to a maid, who ran off immediately to get the pea.

It was brought to the table on a velvet cushion.

"This was the source of your discomfort," the queen explained, putting the pea in the princess's hand. "You are without doubt a real princess," she said. "Nobody else could be quite so sensitive."

The prince and his real princess were married within a month, and the pea was placed in the Royal Museum for all to see.

Unless someone has taken it, you'll find it there still.

THE GRATEFUL PRINCE

The King of Goldland was lost, deep inside a forest. As darkness drew in, he saw a man coming towards him.

"What are you doing here?" asked the stranger. "When night falls the wild beasts will come looking for food."

"I'm lost," replied the king, "and I'm trying to get home."

"Promise me the first thing that comes out of your house and I will show you the way," said the stranger.

The king paused for a moment, thinking of his best hunting dog, who always rushed out of the castle gates to greet him. Could he bear to part with him?

"I'll find my own way out of this forest," he decided.

The stranger nodded and went on his way.

For three days, the king followed path after path, but each led him back to where he began. He was almost in despair when the stranger suddenly appeared once more, blocking his way.

"Promise me the first thing that comes out of your house and I will show you the way," he offered again.

The king refused, but
three more days passed
while he wandered wearily
through the forest. At last he
sank, exhausted, to the ground.

Then, for the third time, the
stranger stood before the king. "Promise me
the first thing that comes out of your house and I
will guide you out of the forest," he said once more.

"I promise," said the king at last. "My kingdom
needs me. Now show me the way."

No sooner had he uttered those words,
than he found himself at the edge of the forest,
with the castle turrets gleaming in the distance.
He began to run. Just as he reached the great
gates, the nurse came out with the royal baby,
who stretched out his arms to him.

The king shrank back, horrified. A moment later, his dog bounded up to greet him.

"Away with you!" cried the king, and sobbing, he rushed inside.

When the shock had passed, he had time to think of a plan. On his orders, his baby boy was exchanged for the daughter of a peasant. For a year, the little prince lived as the son of peasants, while the baby girl slept in a golden cradle, under silken sheets. At the end of a year, the stranger arrived to claim his reward. Believing the baby girl to be the true child of the king, he took her away. The king ordered a feast, delighted that his plan

had worked. He then gave splendid presents to the foster parents, so his son should lack for nothing. But he didn't dare bring back his baby, in case his trick was found out.

The years passed and the boy grew tall and strong. The king told him the secret of his history and it hung like a shadow over him — the thought of the girl, in the hands of a stranger, living somewhere far away. And he promised himself that when he was old enough, he would travel the world, and never rest until he had set her free.

So when he thought himself a man at last, he dressed in his farm clothes, put some peas in his pockets and set out for the forest where his father had lost himself, eighteen years before. As he walked along the winding paths, he cried out, "Oh I am lost! Lost! Where can I be?"

A strange man suddenly appeared before him. "I know this place," he said, "and I can lead you out of it, if you promise me a reward."

"I am only a poor beggar and an orphan," replied the prince. "I have nothing to offer you except my life."

"Then you must work for me," replied the stranger. "For wages, I'll give you food, clothes and a piece of land."

The prince made the deal and followed the strange old man, all the while being careful to drop a pea every now and then. They walked all day, until they came to a large stone. The old man looked around, gave a sharp whistle, then tapped the ground three times with his left foot. A secret door appeared under the stone, which led to the mouth of a cave. The old man seized the prince by the arm. "Follow me!" he said roughly.

The prince went after the stranger into a darkness even deeper than night. After a long while, he thought he saw a glimmer of light, but it was not from the sun or moon, only a kind of pale cloud in a strange underworld.

There were trees and plants, birds and beasts... but nothing like he had ever seen before. And everything was held by a strange stillness. The birds sang, but no sound came out. Water flowed noiselessly over pebbles, the wind bowed the tops of the trees and bees darted about, all without making a sound. The old stranger never said a word, and when the prince tried to ask what was happening, his voice died in his throat. At long last, a faint noise broke his ears and the life of shadows suddenly became real.

"What is this enchanted place?" wondered the prince. "And how will I ever get out?"

The stranger led him to his house and as they stepped over the threshold he saw a beautiful girl, with brown eyes and curly fair hair. Over supper that night, he longed to speak to her, but she never so much as glanced at him.

"For one day you may rest," the stranger said to the prince. "But after that I will show you what work you have to do."

That night, the prince lay awake for a long time. He was sure the girl was the one he was looking for, but how would they escape?

The next day, the prince rambled around the stranger's house. He found a farm beyond it, with a huge white horse, a fat black cow and fields full of long, lush grass.

"I am going to set you an easy task tomorrow," said the old man. "Take this scythe and cut as much grass as the white horse will want for its day's feed. But I had better not come back and find its stall empty. So beware!"

"That doesn't sound too hard," the prince thought. But once the old man had left, the brown-eyed girl came up to him.

"What task has he set you?" she asked.

"Just to cut hay for the horse."

"Then you are doomed," replied the girl. "That horse is ferociously hungry. It takes twenty men a day to feed it. Listen, this is your only chance. When you have filled the stable as full as it will hold, you must weave a strong braid of rushes, and be sure the horse sees what you are doing. When it asks what the braid is for, say, 'With this braid I'll bind the mouth of the one who is too greedy.'"

Early the next morning, the prince set to work. His scythe danced through the grass and soon he had enough to fill the manger. He carried in the first load, but when he returned with the second, he found to his horror that the manger was empty. Then he remembered the girl's advice. He took out the rushes and braided them quickly.

"What are you doing?" asked
the horse.

"Just weaving a strap to bind
the mouth of the one who is too
greedy," replied the prince, airily.

The white horse sighed
deeply when it heard this, and
decided to eat no more that day.

When the old man walked in at
the end of the day, and saw the stall
filled with hay, he looked astonished.

"Who helped you?" he demanded.

"Oh, I had no help," replied the prince.

That evening, his master said,
"Tomorrow I have a special task for you.
Milk the black cow, but make sure it's

milked dry, or it may be the worse for you."

"How hard can that be?" thought the prince. But just as he was going to bed, the brown-eyed girl came to him and asked, "What is your task tomorrow?"

"I have nothing to do all day, except milk the black cow dry," replied the prince.

"Oh, how unlucky you are," replied the girl. "If you were to try from morning till night you couldn't do it. Listen, and I will tell you what to do." And she stood on her tiptoes and whispered into the prince's ear.

As the dawn sky turned to red, the prince jumped out of bed. He went to the cow's stall, and began to do exactly as the girl had told him the evening before.

The black cow watched him in surprise. "What

are you doing?" she said at last.

"Just weaving a strap to bind the feet of one who may not give me enough milk," replied the prince, airily.

The cow sighed deeply and the prince milked her until she ran dry.

Then the old man entered the stall and sat down to milk the cow himself, but there wasn't a drop of milk left. "Who helped you?" he demanded.

"Oh, I had no help," replied the prince.

That night, when the prince went to his master to learn his task for the next day, the old man smiled at him. "I am very pleased with your work," he said. "Come to me at dawn and bring the girl with you. I want to give you both my blessing."

When he told the girl she went white with fear.

"He has found us out," she whispered, "and means to destroy us both. We must escape. First, I must get my things."

Back she came with a bundle, tucked in the crook of her arm.

"What's in it?" asked the prince.

"This land is full of magic," answered the girl. And she peeled back the covers to show a glowing red ball. "We will use this to light our way."

They crept down the dark tunnel until they came to the forest again. As the prince had hoped, the peas he had dropped had taken root and grown into a little hedge, to guide them on their way.

"Where do you come from?" the prince asked as they fled.

The girl shook her head. "I do not know," she

replied. "The old man once told me that I am a king's daughter and that he got me by cunning, but that is all he would say."

The prince was overjoyed to hear her say this. At last, he had set her free. They ran on through the night, and as dawn broke, the old man came looking for them.

When he saw their beds were empty and had not been slept in, he cried out in rage. "I will get them," he thundered. And he summoned the clouds and the wind to help him.

The prince and the girl ran on, until they came to a clearing in the forest. "Something has happened," the girl said suddenly. "The ball is moving in my hand. I'm sure we're being followed!"

Behind them, they saw a black cloud, flying before the wind. Then the girl turned the ball three times in her hand. "Listen to me, my ball, my ball. Be quick and change me into a stream, and this man into a little fish."

In an instant there was a stream with a fish swimming in it. The black cloud hovered over them for a moment, and then returned to the old man.

"What did you see?" the old man asked.

"No man or woman," replied the black cloud. "Only a stream and a fish in it."

"You fool!" roared the old man. "That was them. Go and blow away the stream and catch

the fish."

The black cloud sped back, the wind blowing
fast behind it.

The prince and the girl had reached the
middle of the forest, when the girl stopped again.
"Something has happened," she said. "The ball is
moving in my hand."

Looking around, they saw a cloud flying
towards them, larger and blacker than the first,
and striped with red.

"That is the old man's helper, pursuing us
again," she cried. "And he is even angrier than
before." Then she turned the ball three times in
her hands and said, "Listen to me, my ball, my
ball. Be quick and change us both — me into a
wild rose, and this man into my stem."

An instant later it was done, just as the black

cloud hovered over them, looking eagerly for a stream and a fish. But finding neither, it flew back to the old man.

"Did you find them?" he cried.

"No," replied the black cloud. "There was nothing but a rose, on a single stem, in the middle of the forest."

"Fool!" shouted the old man. "That was them! Bring them to me," he thundered. "Tear up the rose and the roots too, and don't leave anything behind, however strange it may be."

By now, the prince and the girl had reached the darkest part of the forest. Worn out and breathless, they came at last to a large stone. The ball began to move again, trembling in the girl's hands. She bent down and whispered into its glow, "Listen to me, my ball, my ball. Roll the stone to one side so that we may find the way home."

As soon as she spoke, the stone began to move. The prince and the girl found themselves at the edge of the forest, back in their own world.

"We are safe," said the girl. "The old man is a wizard, but he has no power over us here. And now it is time for us to part. You will return to your parents, and I must go in search of mine."

"No!" cried the prince. "I will never part from you. Please — come with me and be my wife. We have escaped from trouble together. Now we can share our joys."

Together, they went to the castle, where the king was the first to greet them. "At last you have come back, my son."

The prince told everyone at the castle how the

girl had been taken many years before, and how
she had saved him. Then they went to the cottage
where the prince had grown up, and the girl was
reunited with her parents. The prince and the girl
were married the next day, with feasting and
laughter and their family around them.

THE PRINCE AND THE PHOENIX

The Prince of Jing dreamed one night of a beautiful princess, sitting in a garden he had never seen before. In his dream, he fell desperately in love with her, and when he woke he cried out at the loss of her. He called for his ink and his brushes and drew her image on a piece of precious silk.

In one corner he wrote the lines:

Her skin is pale as moonlight
Her hair as dark as night
From birth to youth we never met, yet
In my dreams we are together, she and I.

Then he summoned his ministers and
showed them the portrait.
"Can anyone tell me the
name of this beautiful
maiden?" he asked.

The ministers
all shook their
heads and stroked
their beards and
confessed they did
not know her name.

So the prince sent them away in disgrace and began asking everyone in the palace, high or low, if they could name the princess in the picture. One after the other they shook their heads.

The prince then asked the magicians of the kingdom to find out the name of his dream princess. But each one gave a different answer.

"How can I trust you now?" demanded the prince, and banished them from his kingdom.

The portrait was shown around every room in the palace, to every visitor, but all who gazed at that beautiful face shook their heads. They were sorry, but they did not know her name.

The Prince of Jing ate no more and he drank no more. He lost count of where the days ended and the nights began, which way was in and which was out, what was left and what was right.

He spent his time roaming among the
Kunlun Mountains, wracked with
longing and with sorrow.
On one of his
wanderings he came
to the edge of a
precipice. The valley
below was strewn with
rocks and, as the prince
gazed at them, a bird lit like
fire flew towards him. She had curling, tendrilled
tail feathers, eyes that shone like the sun and
wings that spanned the sky.

"I am the phoenix," she announced. "Why is
the mighty Prince of Jing so far from home? Why
is your face in shadow?"

"The tiger can run after the deer in the forest,"

the prince replied. "The eagle can fly over the mountains and plains. But how can I find the one my heart desires?" And he told the bird his story.

"I can help you," replied the phoenix. "I can make myself large enough to carry a town upon my back or small enough to pass through a keyhole, and I know all the princesses in all the palaces of the Earth. Show me the picture, and I will tell you the name of the princess."

"Come then," said the prince, and the phoenix followed him back to the palace. When the prince showed the portrait, the bird became as large as an elephant. "This is the daughter of the King of China. She is just as you have painted her, like a full moon rising under a black cloud. Sit on my back and I will carry you to the place of your dream."

At nightfall, they were flying over the king's

palace above a beautiful garden. And in the garden sat the princess, singing and playing upon a lute. The phoenix swooped down just outside the palace walls and the prince slipped off her back. Then the phoenix showed him how to cut twelve bamboo stems to make a flute, which has a sound sweeter than the evening breeze on a forest stream.

The prince blew gently across the pipes and the princess heard the sound. "I can see nothing but flowers and trees," she cried out. "But this music is the melody of a heart that has suffered sorrow on sorrow, and only a heart full of longing can listen."

At that moment, the phoenix came down from the sky, her feathers like autumn flames, and dropped the prince's painting at her feet.

She gazed in astonishment at her own image. And when she read the lines inscribed, she asked, trembling, "Tell me, Phoenix, who is it that I cannot see, but calls to my heart. Who is it who has never seen me, but knows my face?"

Then the phoenix spoke to her and told her the story of the prince's dream. "I brought him here on my wings. For many days he has longed for this hour. Now, let him see the living image and heal the wound in his heart."

Swift and overpowering is the rush of the waves on the pebbles of the shore, and like a little pebble felt the princess when the Prince of Jing stood before her...

The phoenix lit up the garden with the light of her fiery wings and a breath of love stirred the flowers under the stars.

The prince and the princess were married in the King of China's palace. And the phoenix flew back to the sun, spreading peace in her wake.

THE

CROW

There were once three princesses, young and beautiful and clever. The youngest was also the kindest and gentlest. She liked to wander, and while her older sisters stayed at home, singing and sewing and waiting for princes, the youngest walked over hills and through fields, wherever her feet would take her.

Most of all, she loved to visit a half-ruined castle which stood on the top of a nearby hill. She would clamber over the castle's crumbling walls, and listen to the wind sighing as it slid through cracks in the windowpanes and roamed the empty rooms. Then she would sigh too, imagining how the castle might have been, long ago, before the bats ruled over the Great Hall and when people, rather than owls, claimed the battlements as their own.

But what drew her most of all was a locked door on the third floor. No matter how hard she pushed, it refused to give way. When she bent down to peer through the rusty keyhole, she caught a glimpse of a rug-strewn floor and a golden coverlet on a carved oak bed. *How had one room stayed so grand and fine? And why was it always locked?*

Beyond the castle walls lay an avenue of lime trees, and beyond that a rose garden, now grown wild and straggly. One day, as the princess searched for new blooms among the thorns, a crow came out from under a rose bush. It walked with a limp and she saw that its feathers were ragged and torn.

"Poor thing!" cried the princess, seeing its distress.

The crow turned and looked at her. He cocked his head to one side, then said, "I am not really a crow, but an enchanted prince. A witch cast a spell on me, and now I am doomed to spend my life as a bird. But," he added, his black eyes pleading, "you could save me."

"How?" asked the princess.

"You would have to leave your family and live here, in this ruined castle, in the room behind the locked door. It is furnished, fit for a princess, but you would have to live there, all alone, and promise that no matter what you saw or heard in the night, you would never cry out. If you did, my suffering would only increase."

The kind princess promised at once to help. She said goodbye to her family and friends, then returned to the castle. There, she found the door on the third floor... unlocked at last. Inside, a golden bed stood on a crimson rug, a grandfather clock ticked the time away and a huge stone fireplace loomed over an empty hearth. As the princess stepped inside the room, the door creaked shut behind her. The princess waited, listening to the sigh of the wind roaming through the castle, watching from her window as night crept slowly over the sky. Then she lay down on the golden bed and shut her eyes. But sleep would not come.

As the clock struck midnight, she heard a rustling outside in the passage. A moment later, her door swung open and a swarm of strange creatures swept into the room. The princess pulled the covers over her head. Fear wound its way through her; it wormed its way up from her stomach. But she didn't cry out. *What were the creatures?* She had to know. As the rustling noise came closer, she peered out. Their bodies seemed to be no more than wisps of smoke, but she could see here a bony finger, there yellow teeth in a

wicked smile.

The creatures rushed to the fireplace. "Let's light a fire," they chanted, "till it's spitting and crackling. Fetch a cauldron of water, boiling and bubbling. Fear the creatures of the night, laughing and cackling..."

All at once the creatures turned towards the princess, grasping for her with their bony hands, dragging her towards the fire. The princess caught her cry in her throat and forced it back. She would not break her promise to the crow.

As she neared the bubbling cauldron, panic rising within her, a glimmer of light stole in through the window. The evil spirits wailed, "Here comes the dawn!" and slithered back the way they'd come, out of the door, down the passage, seeking the castle's darkness once more.

The princess stood looking at the empty hearth, at her bare arms, with no marks to show where bony fingers had gripped her.

"Thank you! Thank you!" cried the crow, hopping in through the open door.

And so it went on for a year. The princess was alone by day, but each night the strange creatures came and the princess refused to cry out. And each morning, the crow came in to thank her.

As the months passed, the princess noticed the crow's limp had gone. His feathers were no longer torn, his eyes no longer dull. He took on a glossy sheen, shining like a black pearl.

"I am nearly free from the spell," announced the crow one morning. "Tonight should be my last as a bird. Tomorrow, I will be a prince once more."

That night, the princess waited triumphantly

for the creatures to come. For a year she had been
brave. She could be brave for one night more. As
the clock struck midnight, she listened for the
familiar rustling noise in the passage, but this time
she heard firm footsteps on the stone floor. The
door to her room burst
open and in strode a
witch as tall as the
ceiling. Her hair was
seaweed-green, blue flames
leaped from her eyes and
her tongue was forked like
a snake's.

"It was I who turned the
prince into a crow," she hissed, and the princess
recoiled from her breath. "And I will not allow you
to break my spell."

The witch came closer still. "Scream and I shall go away," she promised. "But if you stay silent..." and she raised her claw-like hands as she spoke.

The princess shut her eyes. She clamped her hands over her ears. She thought of her promise and nothing else. Only when she heard the rooster crow did she dare to open her eyes.

A handsome man stood before her. He knelt at her feet and kissed her hands. "I am the prince," he said. "You have freed me from my suffering as a crow, through your bravery and goodness. Come and see my castle."

He led her out of the room and down the passage. The princess gasped. The crumbling stones and cracked windows had vanished with the witch. As they entered the Great Hall, she saw thick tapestries hanging on the walls. Fires burned in the grates and servants walked the long corridors, carrying plates piled high with food. Everything in the castle was as it had once been. The enchantment was broken.

"Will you live here and be my wife?" asked the prince.

And the princess happily agreed.

CINDERELLA

Once there was a girl named Ella. Her mother was long dead, and her father had remarried. Ella's stepmother was horribly proud and bossy, and she had two even more horribly proud and bossy daughters.

Ella scarcely saw her father any more. He was out all hours working, trying to keep up with his new wife's constant demands.

Poor Ella's life was a misery. Her stepmother and stepsisters treated her like a slave. They made her scrub the floors and wash the pots and pans, clean the windows and sweep the fireplaces. And on top of all that, she had to wait on them hand and foot, answering their every call for cakes or tea, cushions or a footrest. She was so kind and sweet-tempered, that she did everything they asked without a single complaint.

Once when they shouted for her, she came in all black with soot and cinders — she had been in the middle of cleaning the fireplaces. Her stepsisters took one look at her and burst out laughing. "From now on we should call you Cinders," snorted one.

"Let's call her Cinderella," sneered the other.

The name stuck. Before long, Cinderella

couldn't even remember her old name or, for that matter, anything about her old life.

One day, a letter arrived. It was an invitation from the prince himself to a ball at the Royal Palace that evening. Invitations had been sent to every noble house in the kingdom. This was to be an extremely grand party.

Cinderella's stepmother swelled with pride and her stepsisters nearly popped with excitement. They began preening themselves at once. "I shall wear my green lace dress," cooed one. "I shall wear pink velvet," crooned the other, and they both shouted for Cinderella to wash and iron all their petticoats and help them do their hair.

Cinderella rushed about, ironing clothes and polishing necklaces, brushing hair and pinning it up in fancy styles. When she had finished, and her two stepsisters were admiring themselves in the mirror, she asked timidly, "May I come to the ball too?"

"YOU?" screeched her stepsisters together.

"Don't be stupid. Of course not," scoffed one.

"You'd look ridiculous with your sooty face and ragged dress," snorted the other.

So, when the two girls tottered out of the door after their mother to go to the ball, Cinderella stayed behind all alone. She sat on the edge of the hearth in the kitchen, buried her face in her hands, and burst into tears. "Oh, I *wish* I could go to the ball," she sobbed.

Just then, a strange tinkling sound filled the air

and when Cinderella looked up she saw a beautiful lady hovering by the fireplace. Her dress seemed to be covered in sparkling lights, which moved around as Cinderella looked at them, and her feet didn't touch the floor once. In her hand she held a twinkling magic wand.

Cinderella dried her eyes hastily on a rag. "I'm sorry, who are you?" she asked.

"I'm your fairy godmother, my dear," the lady replied. "I knew your mother very well. Now then, what was it you wished for just now?"

"I – I wished I could go to the ball," whispered Cinderella.

The lady smiled kindly. "Well then, dry your tears and cry no more, for you *shall* go to the ball," she announced. Then, in a rather more businesslike tone, she asked, "Do you have any pumpkins in the garden?"

Cinderella thought that a very odd thing to ask, but she answered politely, "Yes, we do," and took the fairy godmother outside to see them.

The lady tapped the largest pumpkin with her wand, and in a flash it turned into a golden coach.

"We need horses to pull it," the fairy godmother said thoughtfully. "Do you have any mousetraps?"

Cinderella nodded, speechless with astonishment, and brought out a trap with six squeaking white mice in it. Her fairy godmother waved her wand and at once they turned into six beautiful white horses, tossing their long manes and stamping their fine hooves.

"Good," said the fairy. "Now we need a coachman. There's a rat hiding behind that cabbage. Ask him to come here, please."

Cinderella did as she was told, and the fat, whiskery rat scurried over and sat down in front of her fairy godmother. In a flash, he was a portly coachman, complete with a whiskery beard. The coachman harnessed the horses to the carriage, and climbed up onto the seat to take the reins.

"Now," said the fairy godmother, "about your dress..." She looked Cinderella up and down thoughtfully for a moment. Then she waved her wand again, and Cinderella's dress was turned into the prettiest ballgown she could ever have imagined. It was as blue as the sky and sparkled all over with silver and gold.

"And your shoes..." said the fairy. Cinderella looked down to find the daintiest pair of glass slippers by her feet. She slipped them on and beamed happily at her fairy godmother. "I don't know how to thank you," she said, and gave the lady a kiss.

"That's all the thanks I need," said her fairy godmother. "Now, before you go, there is something you must know. Before the clock strikes twelve, you *must* leave the ball. For on the stroke of midnight, my magic will fade and everything will turn back to its original state."

Cinderella nodded.

"Off you go, then. Have fun," said her fairy godmother.

Cinderella climbed into the golden carriage and was whisked away to the palace.

Music drifted out of the glowing windows, and crowds of finely dressed people were already there, dancing in pairs and chattering in clusters.

When Cinderella entered, a hush descended on the room. Cinderella didn't know it, but she was the most beautiful girl there. Her eyes sparkled brighter than any of the crystal chandeliers or diamond earrings, and the rosy flush on her cheeks was more delicate than any of the pink roses that decorated the room.

The prince noticed her at once, and asked her to dance. As they whirled around the room, he couldn't take his eyes off her, and all the other guests began to whisper to each other. "Who *is* that girl?" "She's so beautiful!" "I've never seen her before." "Doesn't anyone know where she's from?"

Even Cinderella's own stepsisters didn't recognize her and hissed to one another, "Who on Earth is she?" "Why did she have to come? He'll never dance with us now *she's* here."

They were right. All evening long, the prince only had eyes for Cinderella. They danced and danced until she was dizzy with happiness. But Cinderella was having such fun, the hours flew by. Before she realized how late it was, a clock began to strike twelve.

"Oh," she gasped, staring in horror at the time.

"I have to go, goodbye!" And, as the chimes were still ringing out, she pulled herself free from the prince and ran out of the palace.

"Wait!" called the prince. "I don't even know your name!" He chased after her, but Cinderella was gone. The only sign she had ever been there at all was a single, shining glass slipper lying on the palace steps. In her haste, she had left it behind.

The prince bent and picked up the dainty slipper in his hands. "This shoe belongs to the girl I love," he whispered to himself. "And I will not rest until I find her."

The very next day, the kingdom was in a rush of excitement. The prince, along with one of his footmen, was visiting every single house and asking every young lady to try on the glass slipper. The whisper along the street had it that he was going to marry whoever the shoe would fit, so eager girls were doing all they could to cram a foot into the shoe without cracking it.

When they arrived at Cinderella's house, her stepmother pushed her into the kitchen. "Stay there where you belong," she snapped. "Rustle up some refreshments for the prince." Then she opened the door with a syrupy-sweet smile.

The two stepsisters couldn't wait to try on the shoe. The first squeezed and pushed and pushed and squeezed but her foot was much too big for the slipper.

"Give it to me," said the second, seizing the slipper and forcing her foot into it. But, however hard she pushed, her heel wouldn't fit into the back. "It needs a bit of grease, that's all," she said, peevishly, as the footman tutted and pried the slipper from her foot.

"Is there any other young lady here who could try?" asked the prince.

"No," the sisters said in unison.

Just then, Cinderella walked in carrying a tea tray. The prince stared at her and got to his feet. "What about this young lady?" he asked.

"Oh, it couldn't possibly have been her," said one stepsister.

"She wasn't even there," added the other.

But the prince, who didn't seem to be able to take his eyes off Cinderella, would not be deterred. "Please," he asked her gently, "will you try it on?"

Cinderella carefully put down the tea tray, and then slipped her foot into the gleaming glass slipper. Of course, it was a perfect fit.

"It *was* you," said the prince. "You are every bit as beautiful as I remember. Will you marry me?"

Cinderella's smile lit up the room. "Yes," she said. "I will."

They were married shortly afterwards, and the whole kingdom was invited to their wedding. Even Cinderella's stepsisters came, though they wore grumpy frowns throughout.

PRINCESS NOBODY

nce upon a time, when fairies were much more common than they are today, there lived a king and queen. Their palace was close to Fairy Land and often the elves would cross over the border and come into the king's orchards and gardens. They would climb the hedges and tease the butterflies, while the fairies would loll on the leaves and drink little drops of dew that fell from the petals.

The king and queen were very rich and very fond of each other, but they had no child to take the throne when they were dead and gone. Often the queen said that she wished she had a child, even if it were no bigger than her thumb. But the fairies never heard her, so they never helped her.

Then one day, when the king was out in his garden, he took off his crown, looked around his kingdom and said with a sigh, "Ah! I would give it all for a baby."

No sooner had the king spoken, than a little dwarf hopped up on a frog. He had a droopy red hat, a red cloak and a big moustache. The dwarf tapped him on the leg.

"You shall have a beautiful baby," said the dwarf, "if you give me what I ask."

"I'll give you anything you like," replied the king.

"Then promise to give me Niente," said the dwarf.

"Certainly," said the king (who had no idea what Niente meant). "Erm... how shall I give it to you?"

"I will take it in my own way, on my own day," snapped the dwarf. And with that, he climbed onto his frog, which cleared the garden path with one bound and was soon lost among the flowers.

Soon after that, a war broke out between the giants and the ghouls and the king set out to fight on the side of the giants. When he returned, he heard the bells ringing. "What is it?" he asked, hurrying to his palace.

"The queen has had a baby," replied a courtier. "A baby girl."

The king was overjoyed.

"We had to call her something while you were away," the courtier went on, "so we gave her the Italian name for *nothing*, Niente. The Princess Niente."

When the king heard those words, he remembered his promise to the dwarf, hid his face in his hands and groaned. But he told no one his terrible secret. Instead he went to the queen and kissed her and kissed the baby, who was so beautiful, she was like a fairy's child. She had hair as bright as the sun and was so light she could sit on a flower and not crush it.

And as she grew up, the king and queen noticed how all the birds and butterflies and bees adored her.

For fear of the dwarf, the king made sure she was never called by her real name, but was known to everyone as Princess Nobody. The king at last confided in the Queen of the Water Fairies.

"The dwarf must be one of my people if he rides a frog," she told him. "Just send him to me if he is troublesome."

Meanwhile, Princess Nobody grew up among the birds and the bees and the flowers in the palace gardens, and could not have been happier. Then, on her fourteenth birthday, there came a knock at the palace gates. A porter came out to see a dwarf in a red hat and a red cloak, riding a green frog.

"Tell the king he is wanted," said the dwarf.

When he heard the message, the king came trembling to the door.

"I have come for Niente," said the dwarf.

"You are to go to the Queen of the Water Fairies," replied the king. "She has words to say to you."

The dwarf shook his fist at the king. "I'll have Niente yet," he said, and bounded off to see the Queen of the Water Fairies.

The queen heard the dwarf's tale and flew at once to the king. "I can only help you by making the princess vanish away to Fairy Land," she told him. "I have a bird on whose back she can fly. The dwarf will not get her, but you will never see her again – unless a brave prince with a good heart can find where she is hidden."

The king and queen sent for the princess, and kissed her and wept over her, until the Queen of the Water Fairies placed her on a bluebird's back and flew away with her.

After she left, the whole kingdom was plunged into misery. "There must be a way of getting her back," said the queen. "We must send a prince to find her."

"But who would go searching for a girl they've never seen?" answered the king.

"Never mind; we can only try," said the queen. And she sent out messengers with pictures of the princess everywhere, and proclaimed that the prince who found her and brought her home would be given half the kingdom.

Princes came from all over, intrigued and determined to be the one to find the princess. Together, they set out for Fairy Land.

Now, out of all the gallant princes, there was one ugly one, and the rest laughed at him and called him Prince Comical. But he had a kind heart and as he followed the others through Fairy Land, he noticed three pixies teasing a daddy-long-legs. They had caught hold of one of his legs and were pulling it as hard as they could.

"Go away!" cried Prince Comical, running up to them. "Shoo! Shoo!"

The pixies scattered before him.

"Thank you," said the daddy-long-legs. "You have been very kind. Now tell me, is there anything I can do in return?"

"Could you help me find Princess Niente?"

begged the prince. "I know she is in Fairy Land, but that is all. You go everywhere. Do you know where she is?"

"I don't," replied the daddy-long-legs. "But I will take you to the black beetle. He is the wisest creature in all of Fairy Land."

So saying, the daddy-long-legs led the prince to the black beetle, and put the question to him.

"She's hidden in the Garden Beyond," said the beetle. "She is living there now with the Queen of the Water Fairies."

"The Garden Beyond?" repeated Prince Comical. "How do I get there?"

"First you must pass through the Mushroom Woods. But you will never survive alone – it is a very dangerous place. If you like, I will be your guide."

"Thank you," replied the prince. "But first let me tell the other princes. It's only fair I take them with me."

"You are a true knight," said the black beetle, bowing before him.

Once all the princes had been gathered together, they began their journey into the Mushroom Woods.

"Before we go any further," declared the black beetle, "I must show you something important."

The other princes ignored the beetle, deciding that such a lowly creature could have nothing important to say. But Prince Comical followed the beetle until they came to a large mushroom.

"Climb up and look over," said the beetle.

So the prince climbed up and peered over, and there he saw a fairy, fast asleep.

"Try to wake him," said the beetle. "Just try."
But no matter what the prince did, he couldn't
wake the fairy.

"This is a warning," explained the black
beetle. "You must never go to sleep under a
mushroom in these woods, or you will never wake
until Princess Niente is found. I heard it from
the Queen of the Water Fairies herself."

Then Prince Comical and the black beetle
went back to find the other princes and marched
through the woods until twilight came upon
them. As night spread across the sky, the elves
came out for their dance, and one by one,

the princes joined them.

"No!" cried Prince Comical. "You can't keep up with the elves. Don't dance with them. You will waste the energy you need for our search."

But the other princes ignored him. They danced until midnight, when the elves went to sleep among the branches of the trees, and the princes lay down under a large mushroom.

"You can't sleep there," begged Prince Comical. "You'll never wake!"

"Nonsense," snapped the princes. "*You* may sleep in the open air, if you like. We will make ourselves comfortable *here*."

In the morning, Prince Comical woke and called to his friends. But they didn't answer. He shook them, dragged them and even pulled their hair. Nothing would wake them.

"Hmm," said a bluebird, watching him. "You have gone to a great effort for your friends. As a reward, I will show you the way to Princess Niente. Climb on my back."

Prince Comical did as he was told, and away they flew, for a day and a night, to a green bower, full of fairies and butterflies. This, Prince Comical realized, was the Garden Beyond. And there, with her long yellow hair curling around her, sat Princess Niente. And Prince Comical laid his crown at her feet and knelt on one knee, and asked the princess to marry him. The princess agreed, knowing only the kindest of hearts could have reached her there.

They were married in the Church of the Elves. Glowworms lit the way and all the bells of all the flowers pealed in song. Then they journeyed home to the king and queen, not forgetting to wake all the other princes along the way.

THE THREE ENCHANTED PRINCES

Once, many years ago, three brave princes were in love with three charming princesses. The princesses loved the princes in return and would happily have married them. There was just one problem. The princes had been enchanted, so that they took the shape of animals by day.

The eldest, Emilio, became a
great eagle, with shining feathers
and sharp eyes. His brother,
Solomon, turned into a powerful
stag, with fine antlers and a fearless
heart. And the youngest, Dario, was
transformed into a sleek dolphin, with a merry
smile and a mighty tail.

The princesses didn't mind. "I'd love you in *any*
shape," Princess Evelina told Prince Emilio boldly,
when he confessed the enchantment. And her
sisters Selena and Delfina said the same to
Solomon and Dario.

King Greenbank, the princesses' father, felt
very differently. "You can't marry *animals*," he
snorted. "I don't care if they're princes underneath.
What would people say? I forbid it!"

But the princes were too much in love to give up. Emilio the Eagle called on the birds of the air, from bold blackbirds to mischievous magpies and chattering chaffinches. Together they pecked away all the leaves and blossoms on King Greenbank's trees, so that no fruit could grow.

Solomon the Stag summoned the beasts of the land, from snuffling rabbits to shy moles and sly foxes. Together they dug up King Greenbank's fields, until there was not a blade of grass or corn left anywhere.

And Dario the Dolphin collected the creatures of the sea, from darting fish to dashing eels and splashing seals. Together they made such huge waves around King Greenbank's shores that no boats could put to sea.

In this way, the three princes caused such a commotion that, eventually, the king had to give in and agree to let his daughters marry them.

On the day of the weddings, the queen gave each of her daughters a kiss and a ring with a sparkling green emerald. "To remember Greenbanks," she told them. And then they parted.

The eagle flew Evelina to a magnificent mountain tower, high above the clouds. The stag carried Selena to a wonderful woodland hall, hidden deep among the trees. And the dolphin swam with Delfina far out to sea, to an island palace shining with shells. There they lived in comfort and happiness, like queens. But they did not come back to visit their family, for fear of upsetting their father — and their baby brother, Titus, missed them terribly.

When Titus grew up, he decided to go in search of his sisters. To him, too, the queen gave a ring with a sparkling emerald. "To remember Greenbanks," she told him. And then he set out.

He journeyed across the land, searching high and low, until he came to a mountain where he thought he glimpsed something above the clouds. He climbed up, higher and higher, until he found himself outside a tower of smooth white stone. *Rat-a-tat-tat!* he rapped on the door.

"Who's there?" came a familiar voice. A face looked out — and broke into a delighted smile. "Titus!" It was Evelina. "It must be you, I recognize your ring." She rushed out and gave him a huge hug.

"I hope your husband won't mind my coming," said Titus, nervously.

"I could not mind anything that gave my wife so much happiness," said Emilio, swooping down to join them.

Titus spent a happy few weeks on the mountain. But then he began to think of his other two sisters. "I must find them too," he said. So he took his leave.

Before Titus left, Emilio plucked out a glossy golden feather and gave it to him. "If you are ever in trouble, throw this on the ground and I will come to your aid."

Titus put the feather carefully in his pocket and went on his way. After a long search, he came to a land filled with trees. Through the branches, he spied a building. It was a large hall built of beautifully carved wood, with fruit trees and flowers growing all around.

Hungrily, he reached out a hand to pick an apple... *Snap!*

"Who's there?" called a familiar voice. A face peered out — and laughed with delight. "Little brother!" she said. "It must be you, I can see our mother gave you a ring just like mine."

"Selena!" cried Titus.

Her husband Solomon was just as pleased to see Titus again, and the three of them spent a happy few weeks together.

But Titus had not forgotten Delfina. "I must find her too," he sighed. And so he left.

Before they parted, Solomon pulled out a gleaming red-brown hair and gave it to him. "If you are ever in trouble, throw this on the ground and I will come to your aid."

Now Titus walked on, until he came to the ends of the Earth, where the land meets the sea. Here, he found a boat and set sail.

After several days, he spotted something shining on the horizon. He sailed closer, and found a palace built out of sparkling seashells, the home of Dario and Delfina.

They were as thrilled to see Titus as the others. But after a happy few weeks, Titus began to think of his mother and father. "I must go home before they think they have lost me too!"

As he said goodbye, Dario gave him a silvery fish scale. "If you are ever in trouble, throw this on the ground and I will come to your aid."

Then Titus set off for home. But it was a long journey, and he lost his way in a forest. He pushed between branches and brambles, hoping to find the path out. Instead, the forest became ever thicker and darker — until suddenly, he stumbled into a small clearing.

In the middle of the clearing loomed a high stone tower, surrounded by a moat. A huge, scaly dragon lay coiled around the bottom of the tower, snoring loudly. Its teeth and claws shone wickedly in the dim light.

As Titus stood staring, a girl looked out of the tower. He blinked. In that gloomy place, her beauty was as dazzling as the sun at midday.

"Hey," she called softly, spotting him. "Can you help me? This evil dragon has carried me off from my father, King Brightvale, and is keeping me a prisoner here."

"I'll do my best," Titus answered. The moat was deep, the tower was tall and the dragon terrible... but Titus was brave and he had three magical brothers-in-law he could call upon. "I hope this works!" he muttered, throwing the feather, hair and scale onto the ground.

There was a shimmer like summer rain and the eagle, stag and dolphin appeared together. "We're here. What do you wish us to do?"

"I wish to rescue Princess Brightvale from this dragon," said Titus.

"At once!" they cried. "Troubles, like porridge, are best tackled immediately!"

Emilio flew up to the tower, gently grasped the princess in his powerful talons and carried her across the moat to Titus, who bowed low and offered her his hand. As their fingers met, the dragon woke and roared with fury. It flew straight at them, bellowing fire.

Before it could reach them, Solomon galloped up, tossing his antlers. He caught the dragon and knocked it into the moat. There was an almighty splash and a cloud of billowing steam. When Titus could see again, the dragon was drowned.

Then Dario dived into the water and thrashed his tail, sending great waves washing over the tower, until it tumbled down into the water.

The princess turned to Titus and smiled. "Thank you," she said softly.

"Don't thank me, thank my brothers-in-law," said Titus modestly.

"No, it is *we* who should thank *you*," chimed in three voices. Three *human* voices. Titus tore his gaze away from the princess and saw three handsome young men, animals no longer. "Our enchantment is over. To end it, we had to rescue a king's daughter from great trouble. Now, the spell is broken — thanks to you!"

One after another they embraced Titus and shook hands with the princess, and all was happiness and delight.

Then Titus said, "I wish *all* my family could share in this happiness."

His brothers-in-law nodded. "Let us get our dear wives, your sisters. Then we will come to live with you and your parents, so we can spend all our days together."

Emilio snapped his fingers and a gold coach drawn by six golden lions appeared, and they all took their places in it. The lions were so much faster than horses, it took only a day and a night for them to collect the three princesses and arrive at King Greenbank's castle, where they were soon joined by King Brightvale.

There, to everyone's delight, Prince Titus married Princess Brightvale. The celebrations lasted for days and, such was everyone's joy in being united at last, they soon forgot the troubles of the past.

THE LIGHT PRINCESS

There were once a king and queen who had only one child, the most lovely baby girl. Even when she cried (as even royal babies cry) she was beautiful.

When the time came for the princess to be christened, her proud parents invited everyone who was anyone to the ceremony. But they forgot to invite old Lady Malice, who was a witch, and a sour, spiteful creature. She came anyway, but only for revenge.

Her gift to the young princess was not a kind one. She bent over the princess and hissed:

"Light of spirit, by my charms,
Light of body, every part,
Never weary human arms —
Only crush your parents' heart!"

The queen gave a cry as the baby rose out of her cradle and floated up to the ceiling — for the spell had made her as light as air. There she remained, gurgling and giggling, until a footman brought a ladder to reach her down.

The little princess was now both light of body and light-hearted of spirit, so that she became known as the Light Princess. She never shed another tear, and if anyone else wept, she just wrinkled her nose in pretty perplexity.

From that day on, life in the palace changed utterly. The windows had to be kept closed against the slightest puff of wind. If the Light Princess went out, twenty courtiers went with her, holding twenty silken ropes tied to her gowns, so she would not be blown away.

The king and queen would have grown sad, but the princess was so merry and full of laughter that they could not. But they did worry what would become of her.

The royal advisors suggested she should study sad subjects, to make her solemn, and swallow strange mixtures, to make her heavy, but her mother and father loved her far too much to risk either her health or her happiness.

Only one thing seemed to help, and that was water. The palace was built on the shore of a sparkling mountain lake. One day, the princess tumbled in by accident and discovered, to her amazement, that suddenly she had weight again. Perhaps the water washed away the magic — although only temporarily, for it returned the moment she stepped back onto dry land.

In any case, in the lake she could swim and splash without fear of being blown away. So she went swimming as often as she could, even in the depths of winter, though she did not stay as long when there was ice in the water.

Beyond the lake stood a great forest. One day, a prince from a distant kingdom was hunting among the trees when he got lost. He wandered around until, as the sun was setting, he found himself on the sandy shore of a great lake.

Across the water, he could hear someone... it was the princess, splashing and shrieking with laughter. But the prince thought she was screaming to be rescued. So he tore off his cloak, dived in and brought her, spluttering indignantly, to shore.

No sooner had he laid her on the ground, of course, than she floated up into the air.

He rubbed his eyes in disbelief. "You're flying," he gasped. "Are you some kind of swan?"

"Of course not," laughed the princess. "I'm a princess. Why did you pull me out of the water?" she added a little crossly, clutching a nearby branch to stop herself from floating away.

"Pardon me," he replied politely. "I didn't mean to annoy you."

"Well, put me back!" she insisted.

"Back where?" asked the prince foolishly. He was so smitten by her beauty that he was hardly listening to what she was saying.

"In the water, silly," said the princess.

So the prince took the Light Princess firmly in his arms and turned towards the water...

SPLASH! Cool, crystal water closed around them. "Delightful," sighed the princess, feeling her lightness disappear.

"Mmm yes," agreed the prince, gazing at her face, which shone with even greater beauty in the water.

They swam together until long after the sun had set and the princess had to go home. "Will I see you here tomorrow?" begged the prince.

"Perhaps," said the princess lightly, as she started to swim away.

The prince found a sandy cave by the shore to sleep in. All night long, he dreamed of the princess. In the morning, he waited patiently for her to reappear. As soon as he saw her step onto her balcony, which overlooked the water, he hurried out. The princess climbed carefully down a hanging vine and, with a soft splash and a tinkle of laughter, she was by his side.

So they swam together that day, and many days, in the cool clear water, and were perfectly happy... until one day, the princess noticed a strip of squelching, dark mud along the water's edge.

"That's funny," she thought. "That wasn't there before."

The next day, the strip of mud was wider, while the stream that fed the lake slowed to a trickle and then stopped. Soon there could be no doubt. The lake was rapidly shrinking. And, as the water sank, for the first time the princess's spirits sank too. She did not cry, but she became pale and thin, as if she were wasting away with the lake. The poor prince waited in vain to see her, but she no longer came swimming.

The lake shrank until the sandy shore led only to a sea of mud, covered in floundering fish and flailing eels. No one knew why – no one except the witch who, jealous of the princess's newfound happiness, had cast another spiteful spell.

But every spell has a counter spell.

As the water sank ever lower, it uncovered something gleaming in the mud. The prince squelched over and found a golden plate beside a hole where the last drops were draining away. On the plate were carved some words:

"Death alone from death can save,
If love is strong and love is brave."

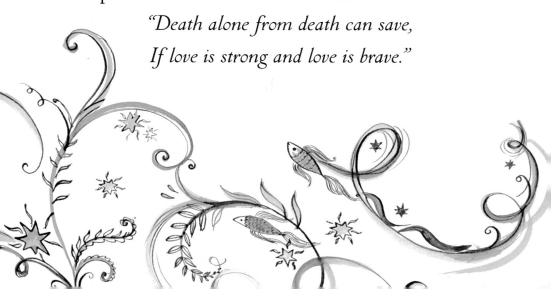

The prince stared. "*I* love the princess," he thought. "Perhaps this means I can save her – but how?" He turned the plate over. There was some more writing on the other side:

"To save the lake, a brave man must stand
In the hole, till water reaches sand."

The prince immediately went to the king and offered to stand in the hole himself.

"If it works, you'll be drowned," cautioned the king.

"If it doesn't work, the princess will die," insisted the prince. He thought of never seeing her again and paled. "It's worth it! Only, please may the princess come and watch me, in case I lose heart when the water gets too high?"

"Of course," agreed the king.

So it was arranged. The prince went back to the

hole and stood in it up to his knees, with pockets full of stones so he would not float away when the water started flowing back in. And the princess watched anxiously from a little boat on the mud, holding tightly onto the sides to keep herself in it.

Slowly, very slowly, the water began to rise. It lapped coldly at the prince's toes and ankles, then his knees, then his waist, lifting the princess's boat off the mud.

The prince began to shiver.

"This is very good of you," said the princess, and he felt much warmer.

The water inched higher. Waves lapped at the prince's neck.

"Will you kiss me goodbye?" he asked the princess. So she did. The prince smiled and let his head fall back. Dark water closed over him. There were a few bubbles and then... nothing.

"No!" shouted the princess, feeling — to her surprise — tears trickling down her cheek.

She could not remember crying before. As her hot tears splashed into the cold lake water, the old witch's spells were finally broken. The lake refilled with a rush, until waves lapped at its sandy edges once more, and the princess staggered under an unfamiliar weight. Her gravity had returned.

Somehow, she managed to heave her heavy limbs out of the boat and into the water... *SPLASH!* Luckily she was still an excellent swimmer. She swam down, tugged the prince out of the hole and hauled him back to the surface. Then she rubbed his face and warmed his hands, and wept over him, until his eyes blinked open.

"Will you marry me?" she whispered.

"Nothing would make me happier," the prince sighed.

A few days later, the two of them married to great rejoicing. Not everything was easy for them.

The princess had to learn to walk without floating, and get used to falling down instead of up. But she didn't mind very much, because she had the prince to teach her.

The lake never shrank again. In fact, it became even deeper and more beautiful than before. The rushing waters had washed away the witch's house and she was never heard of again.

So the prince and princess lived and were happy, and had crowns of gold, and clothes of cloth, and shoes of leather, and children of their own — all with the proper amount of lightness and no more.

THE PRINCE
AND THE
GIANT

In a distant kingdom lived a king with seven sons. One by one, the six older boys had ridden off in search of adventure, but none had come home again. So when it came to the turn of the youngest, Hal, the king didn't want him to go.

"Please," begged Hal. "I want to find my brothers."

The king sighed and shook his head. "What if I lose you too?"

Hal was determined. "I can't stay here forever," he said. "I promise I'll come back!"

In the end, the king was forced to agree. "But I can't spare any more horses," he said grumpily.

So Hal set off on foot, taking only a loaf of bread and a piece of ham for the journey. He had not gone far when he spied an old raven sitting by the side of the road.

"Caw, caw," it croaked. "Can you spare a crust of bread for a hungry old bird?"

Hal broke his loaf in two and crumbled half for the bird.

"Thank you," said the

raven, pecking it up eagerly. "Perhaps one day I will be able to help you in return."

"I don't see how," laughed Hal. "But you're welcome anyway." And he went on his way.

He was crossing a bridge over a river when he saw a huge salmon stranded on a rock. *Flip-flop* it went, as it struggled to get back in the water.

"Can you help me?" it gasped. "I can't breathe."

Hal climbed down and pushed it into the river.

"Thank you," said the salmon, as it splashed in the rushing water. "Perhaps one day I will be able to help you."

Hal shook his head and smiled. "I don't see how, but you're welcome anyway."

Beyond the river, Hal came to a forest. Between the trees stood a grizzled old wolf.

"Grrrrr-eetings," growled the wolf in a low, rumbling voice. "Have you any food for me?"

Hal looked doubtfully in his pockets. Now he had only half a loaf and a piece of ham. But the wolf was so thin, he could see its ribs through its fur. "Here," he sighed, throwing all his food onto the ground. "You need this more than me."

"Thank you," cried the wolf, gobbling it up. With each bite, it grew sleeker and stronger, until it was completely transformed. "Where are you going, prince?" it asked, when it had finished.

"I am looking for my brothers," said Hal.

"Then I can help you," said the wolf. "Climb onto my back and I will take you to them."

So Hal jumped on, and they set off. The wolf

ran as fast as the north wind, across fields and hills, until they reached a huge stone castle.

Around the entrance stood a crowd of stone figures caught in strange poses, as if they had been frozen while fighting or fleeing from something. There were stone soldiers, stone lords and ladies, stone animals... and six stone princes on horseback.

Hal stared. "They look just like my brothers," he exclaimed.

"They *are* your brothers," replied the wolf. "They were turned into stone by a wicked giant, along with all these others. But you can turn them back, with the help of the princess."

"What princess?" said Hal, bewildered.

"He means me," said a musical voice.

Hal looked up. Standing in the castle doorway

was the most beautiful girl he had ever seen.

"Come in," she said, beckoning.

Hal hesitated. "Go on," growled the wolf. "You must kill the giant, but it won't be easy because he keeps his heart in a safe place. She will help you."

Hal followed the princess into an enormous kitchen. "My name is Freya," she began. "The giant turned everyone to stone so he could steal our castle. He only kept me because he wanted a servant..."

She was interrupted by a *thump, thump, thump* that made the floor shake. "He's coming," she gasped. "Quick, hide behind the stove."

Hal was just in time. A moment later, a fierce-looking giant stomped in. He sniffed the air and glared all around. "I smell a man," he barked. "Where is he? I'll eat him for dinner!"

"Oh no, you must be mistaken," said Freya sweetly. "There's no man here, only this delicious beef stew."

She ladled out a steaming bowlful and handed it to the giant, who slurped it up greedily. Then she sighed wistfully.

"What is it?" grunted the giant.

"Dear giant, I wish I could ask you a question," she said innocently.

"Ask it!"

"Where do you keep your heart?"

The giant grinned. "That's a secret! But I suppose there's no harm in telling *you*... It's under that stone in the doorway!"

"How clever," said Freya. "I would never have thought of such a hiding place."

The next day, as soon as the giant went out,

Hal and the princess pulled up the stone. But there was no heart, only a flattened patch of dirt.

"He tricked us!" said Hal.

"We'll have to try again," said Freya. "Quick, help me put back the stone." And she covered it prettily with daffodils and daisies.

The giant frowned when he returned. "What are all these flowers doing here?" he demanded.

"I put them there, because your heart lies there," said Freya softly.

The giant roared with laughter. "Did you believe that?" he guffawed. "Don't be ridiculous!

You think I'd keep my heart in a doorway? No, it's locked up safe in my cupboard — with the key in here!" He patted a jingling pocket.

So the next time the giant went out, Hal and the princess picked the lock with a hairpin and flung the cupboard door wide...

"Empty!" said Hal. "He tricked us again."

"Let's try one more time," said Freya.

So they relocked the cupboard, and Freya arranged bunches of sweet-smelling lilies and lilacs around it.

"Why all the flowers?" the giant wanted to know, when he came home.

"I put them there, because your heart lies inside," said Freya softly.

"You silly, I wouldn't keep it in a cupboard!" snorted the giant. "No, it's somewhere much safer, far away from here!"

"Oh, I hate to think of it out there on its own," sighed Freya. "I wish I knew where it was, so I could give it the care it deserves."

The giant was flattered in spite of himself. "I've tested you enough, my dear, so this time I really *will* tell you. It's in an egg inside a tower, on an island in a lake, many miles from here."

"Third time lucky, I hope," thought Hal, listening. As soon as he could slip away, he said goodbye to Freya and set out to find the lake. The old wolf was waiting for him.

"I know the place you seek," it told Hal, when it heard what the giant had said. "Climb on my back and I will carry you."

Again they raced as fast as the north wind, until they reached a deep, wide lake.

"How will we get across?" asked Hal.

"Hold on tight," said the wolf. It jumped in and swam over to a small island. On the island stood a tower with one high window.

Hal walked around it, puzzled. "There's no door! How will I get the egg?"

"I can help," croaked a voice. It was the raven Hal had fed on his journey.

It flew up to the window and disappeared inside... then reappeared with a large blue egg in its claws, which it dropped into Hal's outstretched hand.

At that moment, far away, the giant felt a lurch in his chest. "My heart!" he howled, and he set off for the lake at a run.

Thump, thump, thump! Giant footsteps shook the ground. Hal couldn't help it, his hand shook too. *Splash!* The egg fell into the lake and disappeared into the depths.

Hal stared after it. "Oh no, now what?"

"I can help," came a watery voice. It was the salmon Hal had saved on his journey. It dived down and resurfaced with the egg in its mouth.

By now, the giant was looming over the lake.

"Quick," yelped the wolf. "Break the egg!"

Hal grabbed it and tried to do as the wolf said. But it was a magical egg and very strong. He squeezed and squeezed, but only succeeded in making the giant bellow with fury. Huge hands reached out to crush Hal...

Terrified, Hal squeezed even harder. *CRACK!* All of a sudden, the egg burst — and the giant fell down dead.

At that moment, the giant's magic vanished too. Back at the castle, the stone figures became living, breathing people once more.

Hal's brothers stretched their stiff limbs and looked around in wonder. "Wh-what happened?" they asked. "Where's the giant?"

"Gone!" answered Princess Freya, happily. "Prince Hal has destroyed his heart and set us all free."

Now the wolf carried Hal back to the castle, and he and his brothers laughed and hugged and talked non-stop, telling each other all about their adventures.

Then they rode back to their father's castle in triumph — the six older brothers on their six horses, and Hal on the wolf. And Freya rode with him, for she and Hal had fallen in love and meant to be married.

The old king was delighted to see all his sons again, and gave the princess and the wolf a royal welcome too. "For without your help," he said, "who knows when I would have seen my sons again. Thank you!"

Then there were feasts and celebrations for that night and many nights after... and for all I know, they may be celebrating still.

SLEEPING BEAUTY

Once upon a time, when there were still fairies to be found in the world, a princess was born. The king and queen had longed for a baby for many years, and were filled with joy. They named their daughter Aurora, and everyone said what a beautiful baby she was.

The king and queen planned a grand christening and invited seven fairies who lived in the kingdom to be Aurora's godmothers.

The christening went wonderfully. But just as everyone was sitting down to a lavish feast, a fairy burst into the hall. She was dressed in black cobwebs from head to toe and looked furious. "You invited every fairy in your kingdom except me!" she screeched at the king.

"How terrible of me. Please accept my deepest apologies," the king said at once. He had never seen her before, which was hardly surprising, since she lived in a black tower in a very remote part of his kingdom and hated parties. But the king's manners were impeccable. "Do join us," he begged, and he got up and laid her a place at the table himself.

The fairy glowered at him as she sat down, and muttered spitefully all through the meal. When it was time for the fairy godmothers to give the baby their gifts, she announced, "I have a gift for the baby too."

The youngest fairy godmother, who had been watching her during dinner, quietly slipped to the back of the line as the fairies went to stand by the crib.

One by one, six fairy godmothers waved their wands above the baby and bestowed their gifts: "Unmatched beauty," "A gentle heart," "A musical ear," "A happy soul," "A witty tongue," "A clear mind."

The watching guests murmured their approval.

But then the angry fairy stepped forward. "Now for my gift," she snarled. "When the

princess is sixteen, she shall prick her finger on a
spinning wheel spindle and DIE!" In the stunned
silence that followed, the cruel fairy shrieked with
laughter, and vanished in a puff of black smoke.

At last, the youngest fairy godmother stepped
forward. "I waited until now, for fear of her spell. I
cannot undo her magic, but I can soften it," she
told the trembling king and queen. "My gift is
this: when the princess pricks her finger, she will
not die, but fall asleep. And she will sleep for one
hundred years without growing older by a single

day. When a prince with a true heart finds her, he will awaken her with a kiss."

Once all the guests had left, the king gave the order for every single spinning wheel in the kingdom to be destroyed. "For if there are no spinning wheel spindles," he reasoned, "my daughter cannot prick her finger on one."

The years went by and the princess grew into a young lady, loved by all who knew her. She was bright, artistic and beautiful, without being the least bit proud or vain. The king and queen could scarcely believe it when the day of her sixteenth birthday arrived.

That morning, the palace was a hive of activity preparing for the princess's party. Teams of cooks were hard at work in the kitchen making dainty pastries, melt-in-the-mouth cookies and the most toweringly tall and sparklingly sweet birthday cake ever created. In the ballroom, footmen and ladies-in-waiting were blowing up hundreds of balloons, and hanging streamers from the chandeliers. In the dressing room, the seamstress was putting the finishing touches to the princess's party dress.

"Keep still, Aurora!" said her mother, as the seamstress sewed a final silk rosebud onto her sleeve. While the queen consulted the seamstress about her own dress, the princess slipped away unnoticed. "My party doesn't start for ages," she thought. "What can I do to pass the time?"

She wandered up staircases and along old, long-neglected corridors, and up further staircases into old, long-forgotten towers, thinking, "I wonder why I've never explored this far before..."

At the very top of one staircase, she found a small door. It creaked as she opened it. Inside, a little old woman dressed in black was working away at a spinning wheel.

"Whatever is that?" Princess Aurora asked in surprise. Because of her father's ban on spinning wheels, she had never seen one before.

"A spinning wheel, child," said the old woman.

"May I have a turn?" asked the princess.

"Of course," said the old woman, with a sly smile. She got up, showed the princess where to sit and said, "You take the wool like this from the spindle, and feed it onto the spinning wheel to make thread."

But as the princess

reached eagerly for the spindle, she pricked her finger. "Ouch!" she exclaimed. At once, she sank to the floor and fell deeply asleep.

The old lady climbed down the stairs, calling for help all the while.

"Postpone the party! Send for the youngest fairy godmother!" shouted the king, while the queen put her sleeping daughter to bed. In all the commotion, the old lady slipped away unnoticed.

"The princess is in an enchanted sleep," the fairy godmother confirmed when she arrived. "She will awaken in a hundred years."

"But by the time she awakes we'll all be dead and gone," cried the queen.

"I've thought of that," said the fairy gently, and she waved her wand, "Sleep, now, sleep."

At once, everyone in the palace fell asleep.

The king put his chin on his chest and began to snore; the queen rested her chin in her hand and closed her eyes; the cooks in the kitchen dozed off as they were piping icing onto the cake; the footmen and ladies-in-waiting fell into a deep slumber wherever they stood. Even the horses in the stables and the dogs in the garden closed their eyes. And the princess's pet cat Fluff curled up on a cushion by her bed.

Within an hour, a forest had sprung up around the palace. It grew thicker and thicker, until only the very tops of the palace towers were visible from the outside. Brambles entwined themselves between the trees, making them impossible to get through, even if anyone had wanted to. The growth of the forest had been so sudden and strange, nobody dared try.

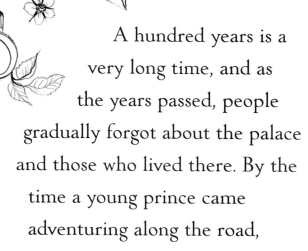

A hundred years is a
very long time, and as
the years passed, people
gradually forgot about the palace
and those who lived there. By the
time a young prince came
adventuring along the road,
everybody who had known the princess was dead.

"I saw the tops of towers in the forest. Is there
some kind of palace there?" he asked people in
the village as he rode by.

"Yes, but a troll lives in it," said a small boy.

"My dad said it was empty," said another.

"No, it's full of ghosts," said an old man.

A little girl looked up at the handsome prince
and said, "My grandma told me there's a beautiful
princess sleeping in there. She's waiting for a brave

prince to go and wake her up."

The prince smiled at her. "Then I shall try my luck," he said, and rode on to the forest.

At the edge of the trees, he got off his horse, drew his sword and began to hack his way through the brambles. Strangely enough, the further he went, the easier it became. The brambles seemed to untangle themselves to allow him to pass, then knot back together behind him.

Before long, the prince reached the gates of the forgotten palace. They swung open, creaking on their hinges from lack of use. He walked into the courtyard past a pair of guards who were leaning against one another, snoring loudly. A spider had spun a pretty web between their muskets.

The prince climbed the palace steps and slipped inside. He crept through the ballroom,

past more ladies and gentlemen sleeping amongst dusty birthday decorations. He tiptoed past the king and queen dozing on their thrones. Then he went up the main staircase, along a corridor and up more stairs, where he found an open door.

Beyond it, the most beautiful girl he had ever seen was lying on a bed, fast asleep. He stared, entranced, at the long, dark eyelashes that rested against her rosy cheeks. Her lips were pink and her shining hair tumbled across the pillow as though she had only just lain down. The prince gently took her hand in his, and kissed it.

The girl opened her eyes, which sparkled so much the prince's heart leaped in his chest. She sat up. "I was just dreaming of you," she said.

"I–I don't think I could ever have dreamed you up," said the prince.

He sat down on the edge
of the princess's bed,
and the two began to
talk. They were still
chatting away two
hours later, as if they
had known each other forever.

Meanwhile, all over the palace, people were
waking up. Guards brushed off their uniforms and
stood up straight, maids and footmen went about
their business, and the cooks in the kitchen
continued icing the birthday cake as if nothing
had happened.

The king adjusted his spectacles and turned to
the queen, who was straightening her crown.
"My dear, I think we may have dropped off for
a moment or two."

"I think it was a little longer than that," said the queen, eyeing the dusty rug. "Shall we see if Aurora has woken up yet?"

The two went upstairs to find their daughter and the prince deep in conversation, their faces alight with happiness.

Princess Aurora introduced the prince to her mother and father, who thanked him warmly for saving their daughter.

"It was my pleasure entirely," said the prince.

"And now, my dear," said the king to Aurora, "it's high time we wished you a happy birthday! Shall we all go downstairs for the party?"

The princess had the best birthday party ever. And, under the watchful care of her doting parents, her seven fairy godmothers and her beloved prince, she lived happily ever after.

ABOUT THE STORIES

People have been telling stories about princes and princesses for hundreds of years. Popular tales, such as *Cinderella,* have been told over and over again, changing a little each time, so there are many different versions around the world today.

Few of the stories were written down, however, until the 17th century, when the French writer, Charles Perrault, began to write his own versions. He published them in 1697, in his book *Tales and Stories of the Past with Morals.*

In the 18th and 19th centuries, the brothers Jacob and Wilhelm Grimm of Germany, and Andrew Lang of Scotland, also began to collect and publish fairy tales. And in Denmark, Hans Christian Andersen started embellishing folk tales and inventing his own.

This book includes many of the best-known stories from their collections, along with a few less familiar tales from around the world.

Cinderella, Sleeping Beauty and *The Ugly Prince* are based on the retellings by Charles Perrault.

The Twelve Dancing Princesses, The Frog Prince and *The Seven Ravens* are based on tales collected by the Brothers Grimm.

The Crow, The Flower Queen's Daughter and *The Grateful Prince* come from Eastern European tales, collected by Andrew Lang; *Princess Nobody* is based on a story written by Andrew Lang himself.

The Princess on the Glass Hill and *The Prince and the Giant* are based on traditional stories from Northern Europe.

Rhodopsis and the Rose-red Slippers is the oldest known version of *Cinderella* and dates from Ancient Egypt.

The Moonlight Princess is based on the oldest known Japanese story, dating from the 10th century.

The Prince and the Phoenix is based on Chinese folklore.

The Three Enchanted Princes comes from an old Italian folk tale.

The Light Princess is a retelling of a story by a 19th century writer, George MacDonald.

The Princess and the Pea is based on the story by Hans Christian Andersen.

ACKNOWLEDGEMENTS

Designed by Sam Whibley

Edited by Lesley Sims

Digital manipulation by Nick Wakeford & John Russell

First published in 2014 by Usborne Publishing Ltd., 83-85 Saffron Hill, London EC1N 8RT, England.
www.usborne.com Copyright © 2014 Usborne Publishing Limited.